A STOLEN HEART

When her coach jolts to an abrupt halt, stopped by a highwayman, Ruth and her companions fear for their lives. But the gentleman robber seeks only to retrieve the papers held by Mr Upton, a business associate of Ruth's guardian; released unharmed, she is haunted by the dark blue eyes of the stranger. Little does she know that the despicable Upton is the man chosen to be her husband — or that one day the owner of those blue eyes will reappear in her life, and steal her heart . . .

VALERIE HOLMES

A
STOLEN
HEART

Complete and Unabridged

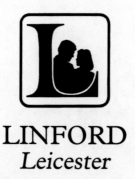

LINFORD
Leicester

First published in Great Britain in 2015

First Linford Edition
published 2015

A catalogue record for this book is available
from the British Library.

ISBN 978–1–4448–2658–6

Published by
F. A. Thorpe (Publishing)
Anstey, Leicestershire

Set by Words & Graphics Ltd.
Anstey, Leicestershire
Printed and bound in Great Britain by
T. J. International Ltd., Padstow, Cornwall

This book is printed on acid-free paper

Prologue

Robert Grentham entered Upton's office above the first fully furnished and well stocked gentlemen's outfitters establishment alongside Gorebeck's newly resurfaced main road. Everything from cravats and jabots to riding attire and dress coats for naval officers were to be provided on request only from the best sources available from York to London — and even, it was claimed, Paris. This last claim was brave as the wars had rumbled on against Napoleon. However, it was made to act like a magnet to bring in the gentry and establish the two gentlemen owners, Mr Grentham and Mr Upton. Assembly rooms and a hotel were to follow; their plan was daring yet simple. They could only envisage a prosperous future ahead of them, and with it, the social standing and power that they craved. They would be the new money in the town and, together, they would be more powerful than the established, over-stretched old money that had founded the ancient market town.

'Excellent, Archibald! This is an ideal location, and I congratulate you on your choice of tailor. You were so fortunate to have acquired his services — and so fresh from London, you say?' Robert looked around him with admiration of what they had achieved so far, as he ventured into the room from the steep stairs to the left of the door.

'Indeed, I have it on good account that he once dressed the Prinny himself.' Archibald wiped a speck of mud from his boot outside the door, before placing his feet on the rich burgundy Indian rug which had been laid inside the room.

'Once?' Robert queried.

'Yes, until he recently fell into debt — gambling. Oh the shame of it, the poison and ruin of many a good man.' He shook his head, then looked up and grinned at his associate. 'Still, best not be glum. His loss — literally our gain, eh? Especially as it was me he lost to.'

The men laughed together. 'You are wicked, Archibald, but extremely resourceful. Did you buy all his debts?'

'Without exception; enough to sustain his services for at least four years.' Archibald opened his desk drawer and pulled out two crystal glasses. 'By then he will have slipped back into old habits . . . Once a gambler always a loser, forever indebted.'

'Good man. I will leave the intricate details to you as you are so accomplished in the field.' Robert looked around the room with its high shelves and empty pigeonholes, all polished to perfection. As yet, only a handful of ledgers and scrolls rested upon the shelves. 'You intend to run all the estates from here?' Robert seated himself on the chair opposite the mahogany desk from where he could glance down through the small, paned bow window and onto the street below.

'Absolutely, Robert. I am installing Josiah Patterson and his son here. The young whippersnapper can do the running of errands and delivering messages, and Patterson will keep the books in order. The business downstairs will take up much of his time and draw true gentlemen in. I have a parlour where a drop of the good stuff can be partaken, and a private room at the back where personal business can be discussed and introductions arranged. We have established a small clientele through our contacts already, and soon, I am sure, more moneyed gentlemen will be tempted to join us.' Upton sat back in his chair looking very satisfied with himself indeed.

'Do you have the deeds ready for my contact Bryant?' Robert asked his colleague.

'Safe and sound they are. I shall take them from the safe and place them inside my overcoat, next to my beating heart. I shall soon take them to Bryant once I set foot in York and complete the exchange there. The investment will go straight towards the mortgage of these fine premises and the purchase of your wife's fine coach. We'll have plenty over to offset the mine and other ventures.'

Robert nodded and looked at Upton seriously. 'This is important. It is the biggest one yet, and will be the making of us. We will rule the whole area. You are sure the deeds cannot be challenged? There was no witness to declare things were not as they should be?'

'You worry needlessly, Robert. Remember my motto: trust Upton.' He poured a brandy for his friend and placed it carefully on the table in front of him.

Robert sipped it and savoured the exquisite flavour. 'You only buy the best, Archibald, but from where?'

'Sources, Robert, secret sources. Best not to ask too many questions; just enjoy the produce and the profit.' He adjusted his cravat. 'Robert, I am doing all of this for a good reason, you understand.'

'Yes, of course I know your reasons. You are established, man. No one would dare to doubt your position here. Look at the development around us; see how the town grows. Much of this is down to our vision and your cunning.'

'Yes, but I need a wife, Robert, like your good self; a woman who knows how to behave in society, of good family, who has some intelligence, but sense enough to know when and how to use it. Not some washed-up on-the-shelf matron. I need a young, pretty wife to bear my sons and to look like a lady befitting a man of my entrepreneurial skills.' He stared pointedly at Robert.

'You want Ruth?'

'Indeed, you have it in one, man. I want Ruth,' Upton said and patted his portly stomach as if he had just eaten a satisfying meal.

Robert stood up. 'She is very different to Eliza. You should be careful what you wish for,' he said and smiled.

'I know what she is and I would have her, mould her, enjoy her and use her skills to aid my purpose. She has a determined and more sober outlook on life. I think her will is stronger too. Her parents' absence has given her a greater independence of thought, not healthy in a young maiden. She is, however, gifted in the arts of a lady, and schooled in etiquette and numbers. That is no bad thing. I will need her to handle some of our clients and possibly entertain their wives. I want a woman who can think clearly when pressed, so she can be of use to us, and linked by association so her conscience is squashed by common sense and a natural desire to survive and thrive. In short, I want Ruth, and no other will do.'

'You deliver the deeds and I shall deliver you Ruth — but it may take a month or so until I can send and receive a letter from her father, who is fighting in Spain. I need to word my message carefully so that her father will give permission for this match . . . unconditionally.'

'The deeds are as good as there.' Archibald drank his brandy in one gulp.

'Then so shall she be. You shall have what you want, Archibald. What more, it is no more than you deserve,'

Robert agreed. He saw the coach pull up outside the building as Upton stood up. He retrieved the documents from his safe and placed them inside the travelling coat he pulled on.

Robert shook Upton's hand, agreeing a deal and sealing a young woman's fate. Or so they thought.

1

'Halt!'

The shout was heard from outside the carriage, bringing it to an unsteady and sudden stop. The horses neighed and the driver swore as his shaken passengers gasped as they were jostled to an abrupt stop.

Ruth nearly slipped off her seat. She looked anxiously at the frightened face of Mrs Fairly, who was sitting next to her. The thin-framed chaperone's fear was easy to read in the woman's pale blue eyes; the unthinkable was happening.

'Dear Lord, save us!' Mrs Fairly exclaimed, dropping her lace-edged kerchief on the coach's floor as she gripped Ruth's arm ever tighter.

'Stand down!' The voice's authority penetrated the coach's interior. The man opposite, a portly gentleman, flushed deeply as he too shifted along the seat with the unusual jostle of the vehicle. Mr Upton stared at his two travelling companions, his expression offering little if no solace to them. His hand grasped at the door handle. Ruth thought he was making to do some brave, danger-defying act of escape, or at least affecting a challenge to the man who had stopped them on the highway — until, that was, he spoke to them in little more than a whisper.

'Ladies, I beg you, do nothing rash or foolish, for your own sake . . . I beseech you. These men are ruthless.' He paused momentarily, and then glanced at Ruth, 'Do whatever the beast asks of you without question — it could save your life. It may be the only way. I will think nothing less of you!' He dabbed his forehead with his sleeve, as he had begun to perspire profusely.

Mrs Fairly gasped, looking fit to faint, but Ruth ignored him with an air of disgust and leaned forward. She drew down the small window as

Upton's grip faltered on the handle of the door, and peered outside the vehicle.

The driver was standing to one side of a man seated upon a chestnut mare. Wearing a blue-grey caped coat and broad black hat, with his face hidden by a black scarf, she hardly needed to see the pistol held in his hand to realise he was a highway robber. Ruth tried not to show her own fear and stared, mesmerised, at the sight. She had read many a tale of highway robbery by the lowly cowardly rabble, or occasionally gentlemen of the road, but had never thought she would encounter such a rogue personally. He looked by his attire as though he fitted the latter of the two types.

'Sit back down, girl! Do you want to draw attention to yourself unnecessarily?' Mrs Fairly exclaimed. 'Let this gentleman out first. Perhaps he can reason with the brute, or be a hero for us and wrestle him to the ground to save us from the plight he so eloquently described.' She did not speak with conviction, more a desperate hope that her words would prompt the man to make a noble attempt at bravery.

Upton looked at her, wide-eyed. Grey marbles, Ruth thought. Lacking depth, but not the cunning to save his own neck. 'That would be unwise and expected. Perhaps the young lady could create a distraction so that we may surprise him . . . or escape and go for help?' He offered the suggestion with no consideration for her safety. Ruth thought 'go' as in 'run away' would be his first thought, and a totally unchivalrous act it would be, more becoming the rogue outside than a man of rank.

Upton's words obviously surprised Mrs Fairly, who opened her mouth to protest but was interrupted as the door was flung open wide by the driver. 'I'm sorry, miss . . . ma'am . . . sir,' he began, looking at each in turn. He spoke nervously and stared directly at Ruth. 'He says you all have to come out and . . . well, best if you just do what the man says. No need for heroics or angry gestures. I'm sure all will be well if you just stay calm and obey him. Remember trinkets may have monetary value, but no value as great as that of your life. He will no doubt want your valuables . . . sorry, miss.' He glanced at her gold cloak pin.

Ruth made to leave first, but the driver gestured that she should not be the first out. Mrs Fairly, visibly shaking, stood unsteadily down from the coach's step. The driver held her hand; she seemed reluctant to let it go. The portly man hesitated to step out, but the driver leaned in and almost grabbed him by the sleeve. 'Sir, I think you should be next!'

Reluctantly, Upton alighted, followed by Ruth with her hood covering much of her head.

'Lie face down on the floor and don't move, man!' the highwayman spoke to the driver, who did as he was bid without hesitation. He then looked at the passengers. 'Young lady, remove

13

your hood!' He pointed the pistol directly at the male passenger, whose right leg had begun to tremble as if it were beyond his control.

'Why should I do anything you order me to when I do not know who addresses me and what business they have disrupting our journey in such a cowardly fashion?' Ruth replied, staring straight at him. Her arrogance was borne of desperation and was a total bluff, but she had learnt at the hands of her first governess never to show fear to a bully, and this man in her opinion was just that.

Again Mrs Fairly grabbed her arm and hissed at her, 'Hold your tongue, Ruth, or we shall perish here for certain.'

Ruth pulled her arm away. She hated thieves, and this man was one of the lowest forms; he preyed on innocent travellers . . . and women.

Sweat was starting to appear on the forehead of the gentleman standing next to her. 'Do whatever he says, girl.

14

Do not provoke him or we shall all die here . . . The man has a gun!' His voice had risen slightly.

'Leave her; she's only a child. Take my purse — it has little enough within it — but spare us our lives,' Mrs Fairly pleaded.

'Miss, I do not wish to steal from ladies. Nor do I wish to prey on children.'

He stared at Ruth, whose cheeks flushed with indignation at his slight. She let her hood fall to her cloaked shoulders over her rich brown locks of hair. 'How gallant!' she exclaimed.

He ignored her open sarcasm. 'Take the folded papers from Mr Upton's inner pocket and his wallet from his coat, and bring them to me — or I will shoot the man dead and have your friend retrieve them from his stinking body.' The voice had a trace of a north-country accent but it was firm, and Ruth was not sure if he would do as he had said or not. She was going to speak again, but the highwayman pre-empted her intention.

'I am aware of your opinion of me. Now if you would hurry, I have other business to attend to.' He waved the pistol slightly in the man's direction, urging her on.

'More people to rob, no doubt,' Ruth muttered in disgust as she walked over to the now shaking man.

'Not the papers!' The man's voice was suddenly pitiful, genuinely desperate even. 'How did you know?' He looked at the mounted man, his disbelief at the turn of events made desperation palpable. Ruth saw the fear grow on his face as the pistol was aligned with the man's head.

'You are not the only rat within your fold, Upton. One day you will swing for your misdeeds.' The rider's voice held open hatred for this over-fed man.

Ruth realised this was more than just highway robbery. Whatever was between these two men was strong and bitter and it was as though she and her chaperone were unfortunate pawns caught between them. They were bystanders and witnesses to something far more complex than simple theft.

She held out her hand to slip it inside his coat, when swiftly Upton grabbed her to him, spinning her around so that her face looked up at the highwayman's. A small pocket pistol was held to her neck.

'Drop your weapon, or I'll shoot her!' the man croaked.

Ruth breathed deeply. Mrs Fairly screamed and promptly fainted upon the driver, who had started to rise, thwarting his attempt to grab the highwayman's reins and unseat him.

'She's innocent — let her go! You would gain nothing from harming her,' the highwayman shouted angrily, obviously frustrated by the turn of events. 'Do you think I would care if you shot her, coward? I would merely shoot you next.'

Ruth stared wide-eyed at the rider, who had spoken with such disgust of her captor. Yet it was he who was the villain. Still, she believed he did care about her safety because his manner had become agitated. It was those papers he sought, not her belongings or the stain of her blood on his conscience.

He turned his horse sideways to them and made as if to ride away. Upton let loose his grip on Ruth's shoulder as he tried to shoot the highwayman in the back, but he was too slow, unlike his intended target. The rider still had his pistol in his hand. He fired and Upton fell. The wound bled, and the driver was quickly up on his feet as the man writhed and groaned.

The highwayman rode at him and pushed him back to the floor with a firm boot. He shouted to Ruth, 'Bring me the papers, miss.'

Ruth bent down and, despite the weak protestations from the injured man, she found the folded parchment tied with a red ribbon and ran a few steps over to the rider, holding it up to him.

He leaned down and pulled her to him by her cloak. 'Today you have done a great deed, miss.' He took the papers from her gloved hand, placing them inside his own coat pockets. For a fleeting moment their eyes looked into each other's. 'My thanks!' he added quietly, and then swiftly rode off.

The driver scrambled for his pistol, but it was too late; the stranger had taken to the forest. Ruth helped Mrs Fairly back into the coach whilst the driver tied some cloth around the injured man's wound. Ruth did not offer any help. Upton had threatened her and placed her in more danger than the highwayman.

The driver helped Upton into the coach as he sheepishly looked at Ruth. 'You were brave, miss, in the extreme. I shall make sure my report records events accurately.' He nodded to her as if his words explained his actions and excused all. 'I acted only to attempt an escape for us all. I never would have hurt you, miss. You must see that my intentions were noble.' The rotund figure on the seat opposite whimpered pathetically as he interrupted his speech. 'And now . . . ' He sniffed. 'I might die for my bravery!'

The driver looked at him. ''Tis only a flesh wound, man.' He had spoken boldly, with open dismay at the man's weakness of character; it was beyond his position to do so, but Upton seemed too crestfallen to care to reprimand him.

'This injury may not be the death of me, but you gave him the papers . . . and they might be. My life's work was in those pages, yet your selfish deed may have destroyed me, miss.' He looked at her as if he expected an apology or understanding. He received neither.

'Shame on you for abusing a young girl so!' chirped up Mrs Fairly.

The driver shut the door, and within moments the coach lurched forward and was on its way once more.

Ruth cupped Mrs Fairly's hand in

hers and stared out of the window, aware that Upton's eyes seemed fixed upon her. She cared not for him or his papers, but was fascinated by the highway robber, who was so selective in his choice of bounty and words. What had he meant, she had 'done a great deed'? He had taken nothing from her, yet she yearned to understand who he was and what he meant.

2

Mrs Fairly entered the home of her daughter, Eliza, in a fine state of nerves. It took two servants plus Eliza and Ruth to calm her enough for her to settle into the prepared room; that and a dose of Cook's relaxing medication, which was administered without resistance. Before long she was taken off into a calm sleep. Ruth did not know what Cook had put in the drink but it had a heady smell, over-layered by a touch of whisky, she suspected.

'So tell me exactly, Ruth, what happened?' Eliza cupped her hand on Ruth's elbow and walked her into the morning room. 'Were you frightened for your life? I'm sure if it had happened to me I should have fainted . . .'

'Your mama did,' Ruth reminded her.

'What happened to Mr Upton? Mama said that he was injured; shot by the highwayman.' Eliza placed her hand upon a crystal decanter and smiled impishly at Ruth. 'Come now, have a little sherry. You must be in quite a state yourself.'

'Really, I'm fine. It was all over so quickly. We left Mr Upton in the town, at the barracks in the care of the surgeon. He needed attending to, although it was really only a graze the bullet made.'

'Only!' Eliza repeated. 'He must have been so brave. Did he stand in front of you to protect Mama's life, and your virtue?' Eliza was seated on the edge of a tapestry covered chair staring at Ruth with anticipation.

'He did no such thing, Eliza,' Ruth began to explain, thinking that her cousin had read far too many novellas and broadsheet reports of these ruffians; although that word did not really describe the man who had stolen Upton's papers or deeds. 'In fact,' Ruth continued, 'it was he who held me with his gun to my throat and offered to

23

shoot me to protect his property. The situation was far from heroic. Upton is claiming to the militia that his swift thinking and reactions saved us all from certain death. He is a liar and a coward and his claims are outrageous!' Ruth protested. 'What is more, your mother and I know it to be so.'

'How could you react so? Mama would not hear a bad word spoken of Mr Upton. He is a family friend of ours, and has some influence.' She looked at Ruth and softened her voice. 'Well, you are safe now and your possessions were not stolen; so perhaps he did do as he said, but you are far too shaken by the whole scenario to appreciate it fully. Mr Upton is held in high regard around here. He is a wealthy merchant who has acquired estates, so I am informed — a *single* wealthy merchant, Ruth. My own dear Robert has often invited him to dine with us. He will have acted nobly to feign a bluff, but of course he had to think quickly and you would be so frightened.' Eliza handed Ruth a small glass of sherry and winked at her.

Ruth was reluctant to take it and glanced nervously at the door.

'It is fine, Ruth. Mama will not wake for a few hours.'

Ruth took the glass and sipped the drink, tasting its quality as it slid down her throat. 'If Upton is single, it is of no surprise or interest to me. How is your own 'dear Robert'?' she asked, wanting to change the subject. She needed time on her own to reflect upon the morning's events.

'He is in marvellous fettle, as always. Last week he bought me a new coach to use for calling on people. It replaces the old one his parents left us. I am to go to the assembly rooms at the end of this month and have ordered three new dresses for the visit. I tell you, Ruth, I could not be happier. We are staying at the Grand Hotel. He positively dotes on me.' She shrugged her shoulders and smiled at Ruth. 'You really should write to your mother and insist she let you come out. By the time they return to this country you shall be an old maid.'

'Eliza! That is too much. Mother has to stay with Father until he returns from Spain next month.' Ruth hated Eliza's persistence that she too should wed. Ruth had no desire to be purchased by a mature suitor in order to have such finery. She wanted a true partner, a love match, like that of her parents.

'I have no idea what your mother was thinking of. A woman should never be at war. It is just so dangerous! Just think what would happen to her if the French were to capture them.' Eliza's words were abrupt and critical, and she hugged herself as if her overdeveloped imagination were in full flight once more. 'They would not treat her honourably.'

'I couldn't disagree with you more. She should be where Father is. She is not at the front of a battlefield, but in a safe area where other officers' wives live. If he needs her . . . *when* he needs her, she will be there for him.' Ruth was proud of them both, but neither would allow her to be out there with them. They were aware of the danger, but would not be separated.

'What of you, Ruth? She should be attending to your needs. Not leaving your well being to my mama.' Eliza looked away quickly as Ruth's eyes stared at her upon hearing her last comment. Did she detect a note of jealousy within her words? Was that her real concern, that Ruth now had her mother's company when once she had?

'You think that we are any safer here, Eliza, when a short journey can put us in such peril?' Ruth added.

'That's nonsense! It was an unlucky event, a coincidence hardly to be repeated. No one was hurt. Mama will have years of mileage from this adventure of yours at every call she makes upon her friends and neighbours. We will be the talk of the area for some months. You must maintain your dignity, that you were unmolested and protected by Mr Upton. Certainly, people will want to hear her first-hand account of it.' Eliza's eyes positively gleamed. 'A lady who has so bravely come face to face with a highwayman! And from what the driver said, he could be a gentleman of the road, and not a common thief.'

The thought made Ruth cringe, as she was finding Eliza's inquisitive nature difficult enough to accept. Contemplating visiting and recounting the event repeatedly to people who were practically strangers to her was not pleasant.

'Did you see his face?' Eliza asked, her curiosity renewed. Ruth began to wish she had not offered a defence of her mother's actions but had remained silent. She should have enquired as to dresses for Eliza's ball. Then she would have listened to her cousin's detailed descriptions of her finery without interruption.

'No, I did not.' Ruth put down her glass and stood up. 'I need to rest now. Excuse me, Eliza, if I return to my room. You are quite correct; I have had quite a shock.' She covered her mouth delicately as she yawned.

'Yes . . . yes, of course. I will let you know when the lieutenant arrives.' Eliza also stood and looked a little sheepish as she spoke.

'Lieutenant?' Ruth looked at her.

'Yes, the driver said that someone from the militia would want to question you. You may be the only one who can identify the highwayman.' Eliza's eyes were alive with curiosity.

'Me? Why should I have seen more than anyone else? There were others present.'

'Well, yes, you of course. Mr Upton told them that you went up close to him, so you must have seen something memorable about him. Just think, Ruth, you could provide the one piece of evidence that could get the blackguard hanged!' Eliza's manner became excited by the daring of her words.

Ruth walked slowly over to the stairs. She placed each foot in turn upon the steps as she remembered those dark blue eyes that had stared into hers. They had been so full of life; could she really be the one to cause them to fail? She doubted it, for no other reason than that he had been courteous to her when Upton had grabbed at her like a ruffian and a coward.

* * *

The coffee house smelt of stale smoke, burning fire, and aromas of the crushed coffee beans mixed with human musk. Samuel entered, tossing the boy two pennies who collected the entrance fees.

He saw his accomplice and friend sitting by the open fire, sucking on a long clay pipe — yet another heady smell that pervaded the room. He pushed and elbowed his way through to him and smiled before sitting on the high-backed settle. He had exchanged the distinctive blue-grey caped coat for a fitted worsted riding coat.

'James.' He made himself comfortable and accepted the hot drink that had already been purchased for him. He sipped it, tasting the brandy and herbs that had been mixed with the coffee as a house special. 'A welcome taste,' he exclaimed, as he saw his friend's smile of relief.

'I was worried for your safety. I heard that a highwayman had shot an innocent man in a private coach, scaring and threatening the two maids who accompanied him. I was fractious at the thought you could have met such a cur yourself.' The man looked impassive despite his words.

'No sign, nor sight of him. Funny, though, I heard it was the man in the coach who was the rogue, and one of the women was a deal older than the other — hardly a maid. I believe that it was the young maid who was endangered by the cowardly man inside the coach . . . so I heard.' He warmed himself by the open fire.

'Whichever tale is true, I am glad you

are here. So how did your business go, Samuel? Did you make good on your investment?' James sucked on his pipe and sat forward as he awaited Samuel's answer.

'Yes,' was the simple reply.

'So?' James looked at him expectantly.

'That is done, no more to say.' Samuel drank more of the liquid and stared at the fire. He saw a flame flicker and dance as it stretched upwards towards the chimney. He thought of the hazel eyes that had been so full of indignation and fiery temperament as they had stared into his, and wondered if they should ever meet under more civil circumstances.

'You brought them with you?' James's voice drifted through his thoughts.

'No. Not here. It would be too dangerous.' Samuel glanced at his friend, whose eyes had focused on a couple of militia men who had just pushed their way into the coffee house.

'Where are they, Samuel? Tell me in

case the soldiers have recognised you.'
James was looking slightly flustered.

Samuel was perfectly calm. 'They're safe, and so am I, as long as only I know where they are.'

James stood up, leaving the pipe on the fire's hearth. He picked up his hat. 'Your arrogance will be your undoing, Samuel. I wish you well. Give them up to a lawyer at your first chance and travel safely.'

He placed his hat, which showed the badge of the militia, upon his head, and shouted at the two soldiers who had entered. They immediately sprang to attention in their officer's presence. 'What have you for me that is so important that you would disturb me at my rest?' he barked.

'We have an injured passenger — a Mr Upton, sir. He wants to see you regarding the highwayman incident and to discuss his continued protection.'

'Does he indeed? Then we'd best see to Mr Upton forthwith.' He marched out and his men followed on behind him. Samuel crossed his legs as he enjoyed the rest of his drink in peace and warmth. He watched the men mount outside and leave. It was only then that he also left via a back door and made his way to the stables. His business was far from finished.

3

The debtors' prison was built like a fortress. Samuel looked up at Clifford's Tower opposite, its ancient stone upon the mound having seen centuries of change. Yet here in York its majesty was lost on Samuel. The prison was successful in its purpose of restricting the inmates from a life where they could enjoy their liberty.

Samuel had no wish to go any nearer than he was. He had risked his neck trying to help his foolish uncle once more and did not want to be closer to the inside of such a place than where he sat and waited. The smell was the only thing that escaped its walls, bringing back unpleasant memories of months spent incarcerated by the French, before he was exchanged and freed with a French officer. He appreciated his liberty very much indeed and was angry that he had had to act in a way that could have taken it from him again.

After some moments passed by, he saw the familiar yet slightly stooped figure emerge from the large doors. They slammed shut behind him, causing the man to visibly shudder. The man, clutching a small bundle of belongings, walked unsteadily away. He looked anxiously around as he left the guards behind. It was only as he passed the corner of the large walls that he saw the gig on which Samuel patiently waited for him. Quickly, he made his way over to it.

'Samuel! You arranged this? You paid my debts in full, but how? Bless you, for you are a guardian angel, which I do not deserve. You have done me a great service. I will never ever do anything like this again . . . I . . . ' He handed the bundle up and Samuel, who had not responded as he listened to the explosion of gratitude that was falling from his uncle's mouth, placed it carefully under the seat as the man climbed up next to him.

'Hold on tight, Uncle. We must make quickly away from here.' Samuel realised the chances of him being recognised were remote or nonexistent, but it was a chance he would not take. The horse he had used for the raid was a fine chestnut, which he had decided to let loose in a field. To sell it would have been to leave an obvious trail back to him. Even so, he needed to be far away from any gaol for his own peace of mind. He was not a natural outlaw — it went against his sense of honour — but sometimes one had to break rules to right dishonourable and unforgivable wrongs.

Samuel was as good as his word and drove away bravely, almost to the point of recklessness, as they made their way along the uneven roads towards the coastal towns. Eventually they stopped at an inn upon the moor road to refresh the horse and to quench their own thirst.

Once seated, finally Samuel was prepared to listen to his uncle's words.

'I've been a fool, Samuel.' The older man looked at the pewter tankard in front of him as he made his self-pitying confession. 'I drank in excess, gambled too much and lost the manor . . . I lost everything; my birthright. I'm ruined.' He allowed his eyes to glance up at Samuel.

'Yes, you did, but you are far from ruined. The deeds of the manor have been placed in the hands of a banking house in Harrogate temporarily. From there, I have made arrangements for them to be transferred to a solicitor and then sold via another establishment. The funds will make their way back to an account in London, which will be held in our joint names, they cannot be withdrawn unless I have countersigned the letter or draft.' Samuel watched as an expression of amazement crossed his uncle's face.

'I don't understand. Upton won them. It was my fault. I don't believe he would give them up willingly or easily . . . How much did it cost you? If you have them, why do we sell them?'

'You were duped, Uncle. Like two others at least that exist to my knowledge. The man must have slipped something into your port. He has accrued two neighbouring estates and has sold them on at huge profit. The man is a leech, but he does not work alone!' He took a drink of his ale.

'I've lost my home. Why have you gone to such lengths to save me, Samuel?' the man asked as his tired face lifted up to his nephew's.

'The transactions will take time. I have already bid for the manor. It will come back to the family, but in the meantime you will be staying with Aunt Gertrude in Piccadilly. The money I spend will be much less than the value. You will gain from this, as you have never looked after the place and prefer to live in town; but I will monitor your spending, Uncle, because you need discipline.'

'No, Samuel, not with Gertie! You should have left me in the debtors' gaol

— it would have been kinder.' The man slammed the tankard down and then laughed as Samuel grinned at him.

'She'll sort out your bad ways and have you back to your old self. By the time you can return home you will appreciate it a deal more. For the time being, I shall take up residence nearby and watch your friend Mr Upton more carefully. I believe he is no more than an agent for someone who has more means and intelligence than he.' Samuel looked out of the window as two militia men arrived. 'We should be going on our way. From Whitby we will take the packet to the Thames. Once you are in residence with Aunt Gertrude, I shall see to acquiring the manor, and return.' Samuel replaced his hat, exchanging a greeting with the two militia men as they left.

'There is no escape then, Sam?' his uncle asked as he climbed back into the gig.

'There is always a choice. You go back to the debtors' gaol or to the poorhouse ... or Aunty Gertrude's. Your choice,' Samuel replied.

'I'm long overdue a visit to Gertie's.' He nodded despondently, accepting his fate, as the gig pulled away.

4

The following day Ruth was informed that the lieutenant from the militia would be arriving to talk to her regarding the incident. She was, they hoped, the only one who might be able to give a valuable piece of evidence, which would help them to identify the highwayman and put her mind at peace. She entered the morning room with her aunt, where an undeniably handsome officer was standing by the warmth of the fire.

'Ladies.' He stood with a straight back, his hat held under his arm. The red jacket with white contrasting braid was immaculately pressed, with gleaming polished buttons. Ruth could not help but notice that he knew how to cut a fine figure. His confidence and relaxed air surprised her as she nervously greeted him.

'Ah, James! How are you, dear?' Mrs

Fairly's warm welcome caused Ruth to look at her rather quickly as this stranger to her was greeted with an uncustomary hug from the normally correct and proper woman.

'It does not go so well, Mrs Fairly. However, I feel much uplifted by seeing you looking in fine health and more youthful than ever.' He winked at her and the older lady blushed, lightly slapping his arm before sitting in one of the fireside chairs.

'Ruth, dear, don't look so shocked. James's family and ours have been close for many years — no, generations. Robert is his uncle by his younger sister. How is she, dear?' Her smile was so sweet it made Ruth look elsewhere.

Ruth had the impression she was asking out of politeness rather than genuine care, but she certainly liked to appeal to a handsome young man, who she no doubt thought was very impressionable and would be easy to manipulate to her will, if necessary.

'Oh, much the same, Aunt; busying

herself in the fashion houses of London whenever she can.' He sat down opposite them on the two-seater sofa.

Mrs Fairly leaned over to Ruth. 'James was brought up by Robert and myself for nearly half of his childhood. His mama was over-indulged by his father, rest his soul. He died in Spain.' She shook her head.

'I am sorry that you have lost your father, lieutenant. Did he die in battle?' Ruth asked, wondering why she had, as she did not wish to intrude upon his personal sadness.

Mrs Fairly laughed. 'Forgive me, James. It is just the thought of Reginald on the battlefield; it presented quite an absurd vision.'

Ruth thought she saw a glint of annoyance in James's eyes. He looked at her. 'He died bravely, doing his duty for king and country, but not actually on the battlefield. His heart gave out under the pressure of the logistics of organising such vast feats of human fortitude and suffering. He was not physically strong enough to fight himself — his chest had always caused him difficulty in breathing whenever in dusty or damp surroundings. However, he was a dedicated and loyal servant of the crown; a man whose intelligence more than compensated for his physical weakness, which was his Achilles heel and his ultimate undoing.' He smiled but his eyes were hard. Mrs Fairley's words had hurt his pride; Ruth could see that plainly even if the more mature woman chose to ignore it.

Mrs Fairly regained her composure and Ruth acknowledged his tribute. 'We all have weaknesses, Lieutenant, as well as our strengths.' She wondered what his were — the memory of his beloved father for one. 'Now, James, how near are you to apprehending the blackguard who threatened our lives? Poor Ruth, to have been exposed to such danger by a highwayman. It is abominable!' She shook her head, her gesture emphasising her disgust.

'Oh, Mama, I am so sorry to be late.

Forgive me, James. You look so well!'
Eliza blustered into the room and
rushed over to them, stopping in front
of her cousin as he rose to greet her.
Mrs Fairly stared on with emotionless
eyes as Ruth witnessed the warmth
between the two.

'Sit down, Eliza, my dear. James is
here on official business and not in a
social capacity. We must answer his
probing questions, no doubt. Oh, when
I think what befell us, we shall be the
talk of the district. However, I will insist
that it is made quite clear that nothing
untoward happened. We cannot have
our reputation sullied by malicious
gossip. The facts should be made
known!'

Eliza hesitated as Mrs Fairly and
Ruth were seated in the two chairs
whilst James had been settled on the
sofa. A look of restrained joy crossed
Eliza's face as she was about to sit next
to him, but Mrs Fairly had other ideas.
'Eliza!' she snapped and stood up. 'Sit
next to Ruth so we may continue our

meeting undisturbed.' She plonked herself down next to James as Eliza obeyed. Ruth saw her eyes meet James's as they were now opposite each other, and also the accompanying look of dismay and resignation cross Mrs Fairly's face. 'James!' she sniffed, and Eliza glanced momentarily down at her delicate hands upon her lap. 'Is he in the gaol or at large?'

James changed position so that he faced Mrs Fairly directly. 'Alas, he eludes us. We have found his horse, bereft of saddle or booty. A fine animal, but one that has been abandoned as if it were of little worth. We have no way of tracing it unless someone declares it to have been stolen. The silence would make me presume that the animal actually belonged to the highwayman. So he is either very rich or has stolen it from a distant place.'

'Booty? He cannot make much from it then, as he did not take any.' Ruth looked at the lieutenant, surprised by his words because the only thing that had been taken was the letters.

'Why, yes, booty. Mr Upton had bankers' notes upon him worth a considerable sum. Then there was the gold pin brooch that the man took from your cloak . . . '

'He stole nothing from me. He merely asked for some letters from Mr Upton's pockets. They did not look like bankers' notes, though . . . resembling more closely official documents. He did not seek purses or wallets, sir.' Ruth could not detect what James was thinking. Did he believe her or not? His eyes were hard and not easy to read.

'How would you know what bankers' notes and such affairs look like?' Mrs Fairly asked abruptly.

'I have seen such things. I was frequently in my father's office with him,' Ruth protested. 'Before they left he showed them to me just in case . . . War is unpredictable . . . ' She swallowed.

'You're only a chit of a girl,' said Mrs Fairly. 'What business have you around such things? Your mama has been so remiss in your upbringing. The ruffian grabbed your cloak. You would not realise if he had stolen your brooch or not, such was the trauma you were suffering.' The woman shook her head again.

Eliza stared at Ruth. 'He grabbed you!' she exclaimed.

'No, he didn't. He may have pulled me closer to his horse so that he could reach the deeds or papers he had come for. I do not think he could possibly have taken my brooch so easily without my knowledge.'

'Can you produce the brooch now? Then perhaps we can ascertain who is right in this matter.' James smiled at her.

Ruth left the room as Eliza instantly took up the conversation with James. For a married lady she seemed to wear her heart on her sleeve where her cousin was concerned — or was she merely very fond of him? Or was it Ruth's imagination, which was starting to play tricks on her instead of the fanciful Eliza? Whatever their relationship, it was clear that Mrs Fairly did not approve of it or their open affection for one another.

Ruth searched thoroughly for the pin brooch, but to no avail. She did not think the man had taken it. She thought perhaps it had fallen off and Upton had seen it missing, presuming it was stolen. Why she did not want to believe he had stolen a precious gift from her mama she did not know, but she didn't.

Reluctantly she returned empty-handed to the room. 'I am sorry, Lieutenant. I cannot find it. Perhaps it fell off when Mr Upton attacked me,' she offered.

'My dear child! You must amend your view of Mr Upton. Saying such things in front of James, whatever will he think?' Mrs Fairly broke in. 'I am sure he acted out of extreme bravery.'

'Mrs Fairly, you fainted with fear. I was the one whose throat he held a pistol to. It did not appear to be a brave gesture from my perspective.' Ruth was defiant, causing Mrs Fairly's face to flush deeply. Eliza sat back in her chair as if watching a skirmish begin with eager eyes.

'Mr Upton is a man who thinks beyond the moment. He had you safely in his arms so that the rogue could not apprehend or mistreat you. Ruth, you shall be most courteous when he dines with us later in the week. His ordeal was far greater, as his gesture caused him to be shot down. He is much shaken by the events. Now, please answer the lieutenant's question.'

Ruth looked at James and silently waited for him to speak directly to her.

'Did you see anything of this highwayman that would help us to identify him, miss?' He was watching her closely, as if trying to judge her in some way.

'I don't think so. I was too frightened by Mr Upton's 'heroic actions' to focus on the man on the horse.' Ruth tried to take the note of sarcasm from her voice, but it was difficult if not impossible.

'Very well, we must try to pick a lead up somewhere to track him down. It will not be easy.' James shrugged, and was about to stand when Mrs Fairly spoke out.

'Wait! Ruth, you handed the man the papers. You must have looked into his face. Did you see the colour of his hair? Did you note the man's eye colour? Did he smell foreign? There must have been a second when you noticed something about him.'

Ruth stared blankly at her, wondering what that meant.

'Did he have any scars?' Eliza chipped in and was greeted by a derisory look from her mother. 'He could be a disgruntled soldier returned from the wars who has forgotten the ways of civilised people.'

James looked at her. 'Did you notice anything about him at all, miss?' he asked.

'He had brown eyes,' she said.

James had stood up. He glanced at

her. 'Brown . . . Are you sure?'

'Yes,' Ruth added with more conviction, unsure as to why she should be lying. But she knew Upton was. Her conscience prickled, knowing that two wrongs did not make it right, but there was more to the highwayman than being a greedy rogue. She strongly suspected Upton knew precisely what the man wanted and why, and like his dishonourable action of using her as his shield to save his own neck, he knew what had driven him to acquire the papers, whatever they were.

'Deep brown eyes, quite small. No visible scars that I could see, but I think possibly dark blond hair. It is difficult to tell because he was quite dirty and smelled foul.'

James's mouth curled up at one side into what she could only presume was a grimace — or was it a stifled grin? 'Very well. I shall let you know if we manage to apprehend him now we have such a distinct description to aid us. Thank you for your time.' He nodded to Ruth and then bid his aunt good day. Ruth excused herself and returned to her room to resume her search for the missing brooch.

5

Once Robert returned home, Eliza regaled him with the whole story of the highwayman who she had romanticised into a fiction beyond the reality. Ruth saw that the man's concern was genuine. He was so enraged that Mrs Fairly, enjoying the attention, had also made it sound far worse than the event actually was. Robert had insisted on seeing Mr Upton personally. It therefore came as no surprise to Ruth that he insisted upon their driver being armed with a pistol. A rifle was hidden under the man's box. With these two deterrents in place it was decided that journeys would be safer. Ruth could not but wonder if the opposite was true for, if the driver had attempted to shoot the highwayman, he would surely have been shot first.

This precaution seemed to appease

Mrs Fairly and calm her nerves, as she had been fretful for days because the trip to the ball was now very near.

Eliza had talked of nothing but the highwayman and the dresses for two whole weeks. Ruth wished she was with her parents where she felt she could have been of use to someone, helping their soldiers recover in their makeshift hospitals, instead of listening to the ranting of Eliza's fertile imagination and her desire to see Ruth wed also. Nothing was further from her mind. Fortunately, no smelly brown-eyed villain had been apprehended. What had happened to the man or his 'booty' she did not know. Yet she could not put him far from her mind or solve the puzzle as to what had happened to her lovely brooch.

★   ★   ★

Upton lay ill abed. He had left strict instructions with his housekeeper, butler and groundsman that, other than the militia and Mr Robert Grentham, no one was to be allowed access to his house; or more specifically to him. He was in his own self-imposed solitary confinement.

Robert galloped down the drive. Archibald could hear the horse's hooves approaching and had his pistol loaded under the covers. Robert entered the house without a word to the servants, the horse left unattended outside for the stable boy to catch and secure. He leaped up the stairs two at a time and arrived at Upton's bedside unannounced and with a gush of cold air as he entered the room with such force of purpose.

Archibald's capped head almost disappeared from sight as the figure approached. His hand, holding up the bedcovers in a tight grip, was shaking.

'Good God, man, what is this?' Robert looked through the dim light to make out the pathetic shape within the bed. The man appeared to hiding under a tapestry bed cover. What protection,

Robert wondered, would that be? He did not envy Ruth's future with such a man as this. It would not play on his mind, though, as such was a woman's lot in life. She would be well fed and clothed, and everything in life came at a price. Upton would be hers, and she was Robert's, to buy this man's knowledge and contacts, which were usually both reliable and profitable.

With his cane extended Robert drew back the thick curtain, letting daylight flood into the dusty room.

'I'll find out who did it. I shall find out who took the papers. I shall . . . '

Robert flung the man's housecoat over the bedcovers. 'You, man, will rise, dress and be about your business. Now is not a time to hide. It is a time to be alert, before we are undone. Have you any notion who this knowledgeable highwayman is?' Robert stared at the bewildered man.

'None. He was well wrapped up and in normal everyday attire. His accent faltered so the voice would not be easy to detect again. His hair and face were covered. Between the peak of his tricorn and the black scarf I could not make out his eye colour. Ruth should be able to though. I'd recognise his horse anywhere . . . a fine chestnut. A truly fine animal, strong too.' He sat up as if offering such information was the vital piece that would unravel the crime.

'That's no bloody use! We can't ask a bloody horse, can we? It's been traced. He'd stolen it from a stud and then turned the animal loose in a field. Did it not occur to you that he chose a memorable mount so that you, who have an interest in the ungainly beasts, would pay more note to the horse's head and fetlocks than its master?' He let out a painful groan as he flung his head back. 'You, sir, have been duped. This man knew what you carried and who you are. He has knowledge of you, which could mean he has some knowledge of my businesses too. Find out who has the deeds. See who claims the ownership of the hall, or who wants to sell it. We will be patient with this. Eventually, the trail will lead back to someone and then we will have our man. Find new prey, and soon, or kiss goodbye to your future betrothal before you have kissed your bride. Do nothing and you will watch our empire crumble, as Napoleon's own surely will.'

'I thought you would be angry with Archibald, Robert.' The man sat up and showed his bandaged arm. 'I was injured,' he said.

'We both have been damaged by this, but we are far from ruined. But listen to me, Upton.' He leaned over the bed, facing his associate.

'Yes, Robert.' Upton swallowed and looked up pathetically into Robert's angry face.

'If I cannot trust you and am ruined by association, it will be you who will take the biggest fall . . . the drop.' Robert stood up and walked towards the door.

'It won't come to that. I'll find the

deeds and the man to blame for their removal. We'll move more quickly in on another. I'm sure it will come good again. Robert, if I do have someone watching me, then can I have your driver accompany me? He seems a resourceful chap.'

'I don't see why not. But Upton, if you want the girl, you secure your future — and soon. I am not a patient man, and I have been duped also — by you, it would appear.'

Robert left, leaving Upton shouting for his butler and swearing profusely.

* * *

Samuel made his way back to Whitby and then on to Gorebeck. The weather had turned cold. In this north Yorkshire market town he would rent a room at the Sun Inn and gradually make his presence known. Arriving as a gentleman traveller, he aimed to find out more about the area as if he were a total stranger, and show an interest in his uncle's manor. His friend Timothy Edwards had gambled away his hard-earned stables in the area to Upton, and a broken soldier injured at Salamanca, Joseph Kyle, never recovered from losing his family's farm. These were men he had fought next to in abominable circumstances the like of which Upton had never seen. All had lost a part of their inheritance to the folly of drink, aided, Samuel was sure, by Upton's ignoble ways.

Samuel rose early so as not to be late. He looked from the inn's window across to the old church beyond the stone bridge. He would make his first public appearance there. He had purchased new attire at the gentlemen's tailors which had newly opened. He was taken by the generosity of the manager with a glass of port on offer. No request appeared too big or small for them to undertake. He had the feeling of his worth being measured along with the fitting for his ordered riding coat. Still taking great care with hat, neckerchief, fitted coat, creased trousers and boots, he collected his silver-topped stick and made his way down into the street as the first carriages arrived and the local people of the town found their way through the lychgate.

Bonnets turned his way and nodded politely. The eyes of maids and matrons alike noted the presence and bearing of the stranger. He was being assessed by those seeking husbands for their daughters. *Good,* he thought, *I shall be welcomed into their homes and society.*

Gentlemen nodded politely. Many were still at war leaving older, younger and those not suitable for fighting behind. Their stares were more curious, holding scrutiny and judgement within their eyes, until they had the chance to ascertain his credentials. That also fitted into his plan and purpose.

'Good morning, sir. Welcome to our humble church.' The vicar held out a friendly firm hand for him to shake.

'Good morning, Reverend. It is a fine

church and a healthy flock by the look.' He glanced around him as people passed by with a greeting to the priest and a courteous acknowledgement to him.

'Well we are prolific, and most of my flock have food in their stomach, which is a happy situation to be in these days. Please, make your way inside where it is slightly warmer. You must excuse me, sir, as it is time I took up my place inside too. Perhaps . . . ' He saw a carriage stop by the gate and a tall man alight from it. 'Ah, the very man himself! Mr Robert Grentham might invite you to join his group, so you are not seated alone. Being a stranger in our small community can put one at odds with the locals.' He winked at him then moved to meet the coach.

Robert had obviously heard his name being mentioned by the priest's clear voice and turned to join them as the driver came to the aid of Mrs Fairly, Eliza, and lastly Ruth. 'I believe we have space upon our pew, sir. First, though, should we introduce ourselves?' He held a gloved hand out to Samuel. 'This is my mother-in-law, Mrs Fairly, followed by my lovely wife, Mrs Eliza Grentham.' He stopped and smiled at her, as she did him. 'Lastly, her companion and good friend, Miss Ruth Grainger.'

'I shall leave you to become acquainted as I really must be about the day's business. Excuse me.' In a flurry of robes the Reverend scurried back into the church.

However, Samuel's attention had fallen upon the familiar coach and the women who had stepped out into the winter sunshine. He shook Grentham's hand. 'I am Mr Samuel Molton, staying at the inn whilst looking to purchase a home within the area, sir.'

'Then after the service, whilst the women gossip, we shall have to become better acquainted. I might be able to help you in your quest.' He looked at the three curious women and, without making further comment, led Samuel into the church. The women exchanged glances at each other before following.

Ruth watched the stranger's back as he made his way into the aisle and seated himself at the end of their usual pew.

She wanted to see his face clearly, for there was something about him that had struck a familiar note with her; yet she could not place him. Eliza's twittering, whispering a myriad of 'what if's and 'do you think he . . . ' questions into her ear, distracted her thoughts to the point that she was heartily glad when silence prevailed and the service began.

6

'Who do you think Mr Molton is?' Eliza whispered as they left the church. 'Or what he is? He could be from a good family of Harrogate, or London even. Did you see the cut of his coat, Mother? If Robert likes him this could be your chance, Ruth!' She dug Ruth in the ribs with her bony elbow. 'He would cut such a fine figure of a husband, and with means too.'

Ruth stifled the reply she wanted to give because she was coming out of church, but indignation showed clearly on her face. Not that Eliza realised this; she was too wrapped up in her latest piece of gossip to notice. She was already waiting for her husband to join her with the new man in the town, obviously enjoying the curious glances from some of her associates.

The three women stood silently

together as Robert strolled over to them with Samuel at his side.

'Remember, Ruth, dignity should be a lady's first thought.' Mrs Fairly sniffed and raised her nose slightly in the air. Meanwhile, Eliza smiled warmly, welcoming her husband and his new acquaintance with perhaps more enthusiasm than dignity would normally allow.

Ruth was feeling far from sociable or jovial. She looked to the road that led away from the town to the open moors and the coast beyond, and visualised what it would be like to be upon a horse heading away from this stifling, narrow-minded family. She desperately wanted to see the open spaces and breathe freely again. To ride off, unchaperoned, unheeded and free.

'That would be delightful, thank you.'

The words had drifted across her. Ruth had no idea to what Mr Molton referred or had accepted. Whatever the offer, Robert slapped his back and had walked with him toward the Sun Inn. Ruth had not even looked at either man as the group had talked.

She now found herself with two women looking at her conspiratorially. 'Well, Ruth, you certainly took my meaning to heart. You gave no sign of interest at all. In fact, dear, you were almost detached. Now when he arrives for dinner you shall be the opposite: a hostess of the first note. Come, we must go and pay a visit to Miss Connelly. There is nothing that the old girl doesn't know about Gorebeck and the people within it.' Eliza and Mrs Fairly took a step away but Ruth did not move.

'I think I would like to stay in church a while longer. I . . . I wish to have some time to myself to think about my father and mother. I need to pray for their safe and speedy return . . . whilst alone, in peace, please. You do understand, don't you?' She attempted an appeasing smile.

'Yes, dear. Quite rightly so. Stay here a while and then join us in her cottage — it is only over there.' Mrs Fairly pointed to the end cottage not twenty yards from where they stood.

Miss Connelly had a good view of the church, the main street and the approaching vehicles on the road. No wonder she missed nothing, Ruth thought.

She went back to the church, wrapping her cloak around her and seated herself back down on the pew. She enjoyed the peace and quiet and admired the stained glass windows, brought to life by a strong autumnal sun. Fleetingly, she thought of her parents and nursed the hurt and emptiness that swept through her. She was aware how important it was not to let it consume her, but she never felt so lonely as when surrounded by the endless empty prattle of her two companions. Ruth placed her hands on the pew at either side and let her head tilt back as she studied the craftsmanship of the carved cross beams above her. Her fingers touched something, and she looked down at the pew to her left. A fine leather glove had been left there.

Picking it up, she inspected the quality and finish. Lined with cashmere . . . exquisite. She loved the feel as she removed her own kid glove and slid her hand into the forgotten accessory. This must belong to Mr Molton, she realised; his hand was substantially larger than her own. She smiled as the end of the fingers flapped as she waved her hand.

It was with a shock and no less feeling of guilt that she was startled when his voice brought her out of her daydreams back to reality.

'I'm so glad it is not lost.' He was standing at the end of the pew. A smile crossed his lips as she quickly, guiltily pulled it from her hand and replaced her own. 'I fear it could be too large for your delicate fingers.'

'You must excuse my curiosity, sir. The lining is of such quality I could not resist feeling it for myself.' Now he grinned openly at her, she blushed even more.

'No need to apologise, Miss Grainger, as you have done it no harm — and myself a service by looking after it for me.' He took it from her, leaning forward. She stood up as he bent toward her, for a moment, a fleeting moment, their eyes looked into each other's and she was taken back in time to another place, another situation; yet the same deep blue eyes met hers. It was undeniable. This stranger was her highwayman. His face became serious, hers awestruck, until Robert's arrival took both of them by surprise.

'Ah, Molton, I see that you have found it, and also Miss Ruth it would appear. What on earth are you doing left here alone, girl? This really will not do.' Robert strode over to them. 'I am shocked. It is just as well that I returned. This could have been a very awkward moment for you, dear.'

Samuel pulled on both gloves, his attention fixed upon his hands. 'She was in no danger from me, I assure you,' he told his new acquaintance, but his eyes met Ruth's as if he was trying to tell her something directly.

'I am sure not, but gossips abound and tongues will wag. Are you all right, Ruth?' Robert asked, as if sensing something was amiss.

'Yes, I was merely saying prayers for Mama and Papa. I thought they might need them, and Mrs Fairly and Eliza have taken to visiting Miss Connelly, their good friend, just opposite the church.' She smiled politely, trying to disguise the mixture of nervous emotions which were running around her mind.

'Oh, that explains it then. I would indeed take sanctuary in here if I were faced with the prospect of one of her teas. We had better rescue them from the old . . . ' He looked around, remembering where he was, and grinned. ' . . . woman.'

'We shall see you this evening then, Samuel, shall we not?'

Samuel glanced at Ruth, his eyes directly appealing to hers. 'I believe so,' he answered politely.

'Good man.' Robert took Ruth's arm. 'We shall return to our humble home once more.'

She nodded and left with him without a backward glance, knowing what she should do, but wondering what in fact she would do.

7

'Apparently, according to Miss Connelly, he is a man of new money who has made a fortune speculating in the colonies and has returned to make his home here.' Mrs Fairly nodded at Eliza and Robert as they sat opposite her and Ruth in the coach. Ruth pretended not to pay any attention to their conversation as they returned to their home on the outskirts of town.

They each looked pointedly at Ruth.

'He appeared to be quite taken by you, Ruth, when you were in conversation with him in the church,' Robert spoke, as he acknowledged Mrs Fairly's inference.

'You were in the church — alone — with this man, Ruth?' Eliza looked shocked.

'I was in a church with him and a member of the clergy, so someone else was also present, Eliza. It was hardly an improper situation.' Ruth flushed slightly, as Mrs Fairly breathed in deeply. She had tried hard not to be outspoken, but Eliza's assumptions and appetite for gossip were too much for her. Robert shook his head and Eliza placed her hand to her lips.

'You should be more careful, my girl. Your reputation could so easily lie in tatters. It is a man that you should be courting, not trouble! What if it had been one of the town gossips who had returned there? Miss Connelly for instance, and not our dear Robert. Think of the scandal you could have caused. Perhaps you will be fortunate and the stranger will realise the delicate situation could have caused you much harm, and will at dinner apologise, or . . . ' She half-smiled.

'Or what? Mrs Fairly, he has nothing to apologise for.' Ruth flushed even more and her voice faltered, lacking conviction, because she realised he had a lot of reasons to apologise to her, but none that they knew — or would ever know — from her lips. Perhaps he might seek to silence her. Now would be a good time to tell Robert the truth. How could she blurt out that the 'gentleman' was a highway robber? However, Ruth did not even try. Instead, she meekly stated, 'We shall have to wait and see. I cannot seek an attachment to someone out of hearsay and gossip. He could be anyone or anything. Why has he returned to these shores?'

'Why would he not?'

Ruth stared out of the window. Her mind was flicking between images of the attractive stranger and that of the highwayman. Their build was the same, as were their eyes. Those eyes . . . She had no doubt it was he. Then she thought of the lieutenant and how she had already told lies to him. She could not rescind her description, falsely given. No one would believe her now. She had never expected to see the man again. So now there was no choice; it would have to be their secret.

She realised the conversation had not abated and reluctantly listened. 'Indeed, we will be acting on your behalf in these issues,' replied Mrs Fairly. 'Ruth, time moves on and, war or no war, these things should be attended to. May I suggest that you think about your future? When we next write to your mama and papa we shall be seeking their consent for us to find a suitor of suitable station for you.'

Ruth opened her mouth to protest, but Robert intervened. 'Do not thank us yet; wait until we have had a reply. It is our duty to see your future is secure. After all, your parents may not return for some years. I shall be in communication with them on your behalf. We must by all means welcome this man into our home, as a neighbourly gesture, whilst he seeks out a new one. However, we should keep your options open. You have only to trust my good judgement. I will find for you someone who has estate, prospects and the ability to keep you in a lifestyle that is no less than you are used to, and hopefully so much more.'

Ruth swallowed and looked down as if contemplating his words. Or was he thinking of a far darker option: the even more negative prospect of them not returning at all? It all seemed so horribly dismal and intrusive of them. 'I know you mean to speak with sincerity, and I appreciate your concern, but I am prepared to wait for my father to return. He will be home soon. The war will be won and we shall be victorious. Then I will discuss my future when my family are one again. Until then I cannot possibly entertain the idea.'

Ruth stared out of the window waiting for harsh words or a rebuke from Eliza, but instead she was surprised when Mrs Fairly took her hand in her own. She felt the soft kidskin glove and heard softly spoken words. 'A noble thought, my dear. We should expect nothing less from my brother's daughter, and it is for this reason that I know you will do what he bids of you. So we shall await his reply.

In the meantime you must not shut yourself away from good society. It would be a tragedy for you and your parents if their only child did not provide grandchildren ... such a shame.' She patted her hand and then released it, saying no more.

8

Samuel was determined to have a ride before he was due to dine at the house of his new acquaintance. Not only had Robert insisted he eat with them, but he had also insisted he should stay with them whilst he found a suitable property. This was genuine hospitality which was commonplace amongst those who had wealth. It would be disingenuous to refuse, so he had packed his bag in readiness for the coach's arrival later in the day. Meanwhile, he would do a reconnaissance of the town and area.

★ ★ ★

'Mr Molton,' the familiar voice greeted him. 'Welcome to Gorebeck. May I offer you a drink or refreshment?' James held a hand of welcome out to Samuel as the man walked from the inn's doorway. It was a formal gesture that had been noticed and witnessed by certain ladies of the town, including the elderly but alert Miss Connelly. 'Please allow me to introduce myself. I am Lieutenant James Walker, sir.'

'That is very generous of you, but I have already partaken of my breakfast. However, Lieutenant, I am pleased to make your acquaintance. You seem to have me at a disadvantage, sir, as you already know my name.' Samuel looked at him with an air of gentle puzzlement.

They moved to one side of the inn's doorway to allow the older lady to make her way past them. She stopped for a moment to look for something in her basket.

'Yes, Mr Molton, I do, but only because I understand we are to dine together this evening at the Grenthams' house. They are good friends of mine, and Robert was so good as to come by my office this morning after church to invite me.'

He smiled at Miss Connelly, who

nodded shyly, before continuing at a steady pace along the raised pavement which lined one side of the new street. The dirty earthen road was lined by low cottages on the other side until the road itself improved beyond the bridge over the river.

The mills a few miles further along its banks painted a much duller and blacker scene. Here Gorebeck housed the owners, along with landowners and new businesses. This market town attracted more money, people and therefore growth, than many of the surrounding villages and towns. It was a crossroads between north and south, east and west, joining country moor and dale to coastal roads, and with the history of a market town that went back generations.

The lieutenant glanced at his friend as he strode along the main street towards the stables. Before they turned from the road, he glanced around to see that Miss Connelly had already stopped to talk to another lady outside the linen-draper's establishment. His dinner arrangements were already public knowledge.

'Should we ride, Lieutenant?' Samuel asked.

'Yes, this is a small town, Samuel, with the same mentality. Any news is a breath of fresh air to the humdrum routine of life here, for idle hands.'

'Then let us make more news!'

The two men had their horses saddled. The women waved a delicate acknowledgement as they appeared on their mounts through the archway at the side of the inn and rode out over the bridge.

'Fresh air!' Samuel exclaimed. He looked up at the autumnal sun, loving the feel of it on his face.

'You've changed, Samuel.' James stared at his friend. 'At least you came back unscarred from your ordeal.' He laughed.

'Some scars cannot be seen, James.' He walked his horse on. 'Tell me about Upton and the young woman, Miss Ruth Grainger.'

James was content to change the

subject if Samuel did not wish to speak of his incarceration in the French gaol. He had never seen action in war, but had his own duties to perform at home in case Boney crossed the channel. Then he'd fight him on his own land. The thought always filled James with a sense of pride and, in a way, longing.

'Upton moved to this area five years ago. In that time he has grown in wealth and girth. He frequently visits York, Harrogate and London. Gambling seems to be his main occupation. He owns a mill near Skipton and has other properties, including stables that he is using to breed racing stock, we are informed. He wishes to have a winner at York, his most recent venture being the outfitters in town.'

This last piece of information surprised Samuel, and yet in a strange way it appeared to be one more part of a puzzle that had not fallen into place yet. 'So who backed him initially, James, and how do we stop the man from procuring property by trickery or daylight robbery?' He stopped his horse and looked at his friend. They had first met at school and had challenged and competed with each other throughout their time there. Ultimately, each followed their own calling, one to war and one to protect his own shores, having lost his father in France; his mother did not wish to see her son share the same fate.

'That I do not know. But Samuel, he has barely left his rooms in the town since the robbery unless by carriage and with acquaintances. Whoever had paid for those deeds cannot be pleased with him. His bravado at his own 'bravery' is hiding genuine distress. I feel that he is severely out of profit or luck.' He laughed. 'Perhaps he will be a broken man before you have the chance to finish the job.'

Samuel looked at him seriously, without commenting. He had seen men, better men than Upton, broken. He did not relish doing the same to anyone, but justice had to be done before Upton robbed from any other gullible souls. 'So what do you know of the attractive Miss Ruth Grainger?'

'Aha! Now there is an interesting lady, if ever there was. Our pretty main witness to the brute of a highwayman who had no recollection of any details of him, yet then did.' He shook his head. 'I fear she has lost her senses.'

'How so?' Samuel asked.

'She could not remember accurately the highwayman's eye colour, his smell or general appearance. It would appear her wits were not about her, or perhaps the blackguard stole more than just her brooch.' James grinned.

'I stole nothing but the papers. I did not take anything from the women!' Samuel was adamant.

'Upton told me you stole the girl's gold cloak pin. She was surprised also, but could not produce it when I asked her to.'

'What game does he play? He must have taken it when he held her.' Samuel was disgusted by the man's lowliness.

'Well, I do not think she knows Robert's intentions yet, but he will see her matched to Upton.'

'That's preposterous! She is young and attractive, and he's an old — '

'It has been done many times to secure family wealth. Don't be so naive, man.'

Samuel breathed in, not wanting to pursue the subject further. 'You said that the brooch was not the only thing taken. What else do you think I stole from her, James?'

James' eyes gleamed. 'Why, her heart, of course.'

'Why would you say such a thing?' Samuel asked.

'Because when she did recall the eye colour, it was the opposite of the truth. Your dress and filthy appearance stand as opposed to your normal good dress sense, and she hates Upton with a vengeance for what he did to her. She is no fool and she protected you.'

Samuel laughed at his words. 'You are as fanciful as your cousin, James.

Good day.' He rode on before he could betray his own interest in asking for information about her. The thought of Upton gaining such a prize galled him. He now knew he would, and could, break the man before he would have the chance to damage Miss Ruth Grainger's daring spirit and young beauty.

9

The ladies had retired to their rooms by three in the afternoon to prepare for their dinner guests, who would be arriving at six. Mrs Fairly had been adamant, and overruled Robert's preference for a meal to begin at eight. She held that it should be no later or it was too hard on her constitution, so fashion was bypassed in favour of practicality and her bodily functions. 'Otherwise, my dears, you shall have to continue without me and I shall have a tray brought to my room. I should hate to inconvenience anyone's plans on my behalf.'

Eliza immediately glared at Robert who, having partaken of a hefty luncheon already, smiled, acknowledging defeat and accepting that today would be a day in which he ate more than his fill.

'We would not hear of it, Mother,' Eliza said.

'Indeed not,' Robert agreed. 'What would we do for conversation without your contribution to the evening's entertainment? Six it is then.' Robert left them to try to sleep off his earlier gluttony.

Eliza stood up. 'Mama let us prepare for this evening. I shall have Mary come up to our rooms.'

Mrs Fairly rose and enthusiastically walked with Eliza towards the door. She glanced back at Ruth, who had hesitated. 'Do you require a maid to assist you, dear?'

'Later, Mrs Fairly, please. If she could come to me an hour before we are due in the drawing room, I would be very grateful for the help.'

'Of course, Ruth. She should be free by then. You want to make a really good impression. I'll have a bath prepared for you in an hour's time. Mary will see to you.'

Ruth smiled and also headed to her room, but was annoyed that she was to be bathed and preened for the marriage

91

market. What a choice of a match; either Upton or the highwayman. Strange that no one had suggested the lieutenant. She put on her walking coat, changing her pumps for comfortable boots and hat. It would not take her three hours to prepare for the evening. Before she was cloistered with Robert, Eliza, Mrs Fairly, a lieutenant and a highwayman, and possibly the horrid man Upton, she was determined to breathe some much-needed fresh air. She wondered if he had recognised the stranger also.

She walked briskly to the rise of the hill. Knowing a bath awaited upon her return, she was adamant that she would go for a challenging perambulation. The grounds had been landscaped around a lake, making the most of its natural form. This was a tamed area surrounded by wild moor, but sheltered in a vale. The town began at its edge, continuing for nearly a mile in linear fashion, the only exception being the crossroads by the river bridge. Decent people were careful where they ventured on these paths, as the asylum lay half a mile north and the barracks and gaol half a mile south. It was said amongst the townspeople that if the old market town grew at its current rate, both asylum and gaol would be part of the main town in only a year or two.

Ruth knew she would invite even more criticism about herself and her behaviour if she were seen venturing off on her own, but she needed time to think before the stranger arrived in Robert's carriage. It did not occur to her for one moment that the rider approaching through the woods towards her could be he, until of course she entered the pathway along the crest of the hill lined by the trees, and he came into full view.

He stopped the horse as she appeared ahead of him on the path. There was but a six-foot distance between them. Both stared at the other as if equally shocked by the other's sudden appearance.

Ruth held her coat's skirt in both hands and lifted it slightly as she turned to make a quick descent back through the trees.

'Please don't go, miss.' His voice, the same voice that had ordered her to retrieve the papers, stopped her momentarily as she looked back at him. He had dismounted and was holding his horse's reins casually in his left hand.

'You startled me.' Ruth released her coat and stood straight. There was no point in running; he was stronger, fitter, and dressed more appropriately for a chase than she.

'I am sorry. I have never meant to cause you any harm.' He was staring at her, his words carrying a meaning beyond the obvious.

'Never, sir? Not even when you have carried a pistol and hidden behind a mask?' She had spoken the words that framed in her mind. They hung in the air between them, and Ruth had no idea if she had made the most foolhardy mistake of her life.

'Especially then. I am beholden to you for passing me the deeds and for the silence of your tongue at my return. Many a wench would have cried out; and even if I had been freed for lack of evidence, a brief journey to gaol would have been certain.' He looked at the reins in his hand.

'Why, then?' she asked, and took two steps toward him. 'Why does a man of education and apparent means risk his life and liberty on such a rakish act? To retrieve what — papers? Are you bored of sport, sir?'

'No, I am never bored. Regarding the papers, I am afraid that I cannot say, but I assure you I am not what you believe me to be.' He looked at her, with now no more than a foot between them, as he had slowly stepped forward, closing the void; yet she had hardly realised, as her eyes were so fixed upon his.

'I do not know what to think you are, sir. I would ask, though, that if you have dishonourable desires upon my family or their estate, that you leave now. I would hate to have to report you to the lieutenant, who is also coming to dine this evening.' She tried to leave the open threat sternly between them but he looked into her eyes and both knew she would not do that.

He grinned at her. 'My foul breath and eye colour having undergone a complete change from your given description. This could be problematic for you, could it not, if you wish to be taken seriously?' His posture was relaxed.

'How do you know that?' she asked.

'I enquired as to the highwayman's description.' He looked at her curiously. 'Tell me, why did you lie and protect me?'

Ruth blushed. How could she tell him that she had no idea why she had? 'I . . . I was unsure . . . '

'Poppycock! You recognised me straight away. Be honest, Ruth. You followed your instinct, which has not played you false. But now you must stick by your words, your given description, and forget you have seen me before. We shall meet at dinner as Mr Samuel and Miss Ruth, under the scrutiny of your family.'

'Are you really called Samuel?' She looked up at him and he smiled reassuringly at her.

'I am. I shall be myself this evening, as I hope you will.'

'Do you have debts, sir?' Ruth stared at him, trying to fathom why this man turned to highway robbery.

'No, Ruth. Nor are my funds stolen or from contraband. I am a man of means and have no need to beg, borrow or steal. I merely retrieved something that had fallen into hands that had no right to it. Now I have already said too much to you on this.'

'Then why did you?' she asked quickly.

He placed his right hand on her shoulder. Ruth stood still, determined not to show fear, yet strangely liking the intrusive feeling of intimacy.

'I shall say no more on the matter than to offer one final explanation for my redemption. I was not stealing, but returning a mislaid document to its rightful owner.' As if realising where his hand was, he removed it. 'Sorry . . . I did not mean to intimidate you. I apologise.'

'You did not. So my instincts regarding Mr Upton are true also. I do not trust him. If I can help you in your quest, sir, I shall be pleased to. He is an abhorrent coward. I cannot stand the man.'

'My quest?' He mounted his horse.

'Yes, you clearly have one. Tell me, sir, did you take my brooch?' Ruth saw his brow furrow.

'No, miss, I didn't.' He seemed to think for a moment. 'I wonder if Upton has it.'

'Someone did. I fear it was Upton, yet I do not know why. It would not be of any great value.' Ruth stepped back. 'But I was fond of it.'

'Ride with me to the end of the woods?' he asked, smiling broadly at her. 'No one will see us.'

'That is very bold of you, and it

would be equally brazen of me to accept, wouldn't it?' Ruth also smiled, looking at the fine animal and its rider.

'I know, but it would also be fun, would it not?' He offered her his hand.

'Just a little of the way, perhaps. It is some time since I have had the freedom to ride in the country.' She placed her boot in his stirrup and seated herself behind him.

'Hold on tightly.'

He kicked the horse on and it cantered down the wooded lane at the other side of the rise. Sheltered from both onlookers and the elements, she revelled in the feeling of freedom as she held on to the stranger. She remembered a time when she was small and her father let her ride in front of him; a time of joy and freedom before the war and before she had grown into a young woman. The path narrowed and the horse walked down to the edge of the woods by the lake.

Keeping to the shadows, he said softly to her, 'Slip off here.'

Ruth did, feeling the heat in her cheeks. It had been so invigorating, brash and enjoyable; she only felt the full force of guilt when he slid down in front of her and steadied himself by holding her waist. He soon let go, and calmed the horse, whilst standing happily next to her.

'You have no need to fear me, miss. Watch Upton, though. He has designs on you, and also for increasing his fortunes. You would be, like your brooch, one more trinket for him to possess. I should hate to see that happen. I believe you to be able to make a far more worthy match.'

'He will never be anything to me. My father would never allow such a match to be made.' She stopped, remembering the letter that was to be sent to her parents. A trap! 'More worthy?' she repeated, and stroked the horse's side, as things were falling into place in her mind. Mr Grentham was going to twist her father's words. She must write to him soon.

'Yes.' He looked at her as his hand almost touched hers.

'Do you consider yourself more worthy, Samuel?' she asked.

'Definitely.' He let his hand slide over hers as he stroked the animal.

She laughed and withdrew her own. 'I must return, sir. You are not a good influence. Indeed I believe you are flirtatious. Mrs Fairly would not approve of my own, or your behaviour. However, you ride well.'

'So do you. Until dinner . . . ' He bowed, whilst still holding the horse's reins.

'Sir.' She dipped a curtsy before boldly walking across the open lawn back towards the house with her head held high, a healthy rather than an embarrassed colour in her cheeks, and more than a niggling feeling of guilt at her impropriety gnawing at her heart. She was aware of one more emotion that had stirred another dangerous one, which lingered and burned within her: excitement. It was a pleasant change from the growing anger and resentment she felt every time Upton's name was mentioned. With it was a growing hunger, a desire for more of Samuel's company and touch.

10

The candle's reflection glistened in the two small crystal chandeliers which hung from the pale blue painted ceiling in the drawing room. It was a lovely sight to Ruth, although she was careful not to stand directly under them for fear of a drip of wax landing upon her.

'They are delightful, Eliza,' Ruth commented as she gazed up at them.

'They came all the way from Newcastle. I think they will be spoken about at the assembly rooms at the dance next weekend, for few other houses have two such fine examples in one room.' Eliza's obvious display of pride made her face light up almost in shining competition with the chandeliers.

'Ruth, how pretty you look!' Robert entered the room, acknowledging his wife and mother-in-law, but walking directly over to Ruth. 'Lemon becomes you, and such delicate lace. I should think you will impress our guests greatly this evening.'

'Why thank you, Robert, but I fear Eliza's recital on the pianoforte will be the highlight of the evening.' Ruth was pleased to pass on praise elsewhere, because she had hoped to make her way quietly through the evening, observing Samuel at a distance, after her rather foolish and brazen behaviour in the woods.

'We shall have to share the limelight, my dear. You shall play also, and sing at least one song.' Robert looked to Mrs Fairly, who instantly took her cue to insist upon his request being enforced.

'It would be disingenuous of us not to let you perform to our guests.' Mrs Fairly looked sternly at her.

'Really, I don't mind, and Eliza is so accomplished that my talent would pale in comparison.' Ruth tried to look humble, although she knew she could sing and play with confidence, better than her cousin's more rigid ability. She lacked a natural flow and understanding of the music itself, which Ruth found naturally.

An announcement was made as a coach arrived. 'The lieutenant, sir, with a Mr Samuel Molton.'

'Has he brought his baggage, Stills?' Robert asked, and Ruth looked on, presuming he spoke about their family friend, James.

'I have sent Mr Molton's things up to his room, sir, which has been nicely aired and warmed. I think he will be very comfortable there.'

'Grand, absolutely grand, Stills.' Robert walked over as James and Samuel entered the room; James in his finest dress uniform, athletic and tall, and Samuel an equally attractive figure in less formal dinner attire, his black dinner jacket contrasting with James's uniform. Eliza was at James's side straight away, with her husband shadowing her.

'You look delightful, Eliza,' James remarked casually.

Ruth could not see Robert's face, but noticed he flexed his fingers after James spoke. The man knew his wife admired the younger, handsome man and it amazed Ruth that she still openly showed affection for him in front of her husband. It was either an ill judgement or a moment she might well regret.

Then her own eyes met Samuel's. She remembered the feeling of exhilaration as they rode together through the woodland and wished they could just leave again today. A smile crossed his face, as if he too was remembering the same thing.

Mrs Fairly cupped her elbow and approached the small group. 'Mr Molton — Samuel — you remember Miss Ruth Grainger.' She presented Ruth to him and a polite exchange followed.

'Indeed, I could not forget such a beautiful young lady.' Samuel smiled at Mrs Fairly, who obviously approved of his comment.

'How do you find Gorebeck, sir?' Ruth asked as Eliza and James continued their conversation, moving toward the fireplace.

Robert spoke quietly to Mrs Fairly and they too stepped away. Ruth wondered if it was to be so straightforward. Surely, if Robert wanted her to match to Upton, he would not allow her to speak openly to Samuel in such a fashion.

'I find it an interesting town with some very interesting people it, Ruth.' He was not whispering, but addressing his comments to her directly.

The conversation between Robert and Mrs Fairly had become more animated, as he appeared to be explaining something to her which was perhaps a surprise judging by her expression. Meanwhile, James and Eliza were lost in each other's banter, leaving Samuel and Ruth able to have their own relaxed conversation for a few moments, whilst sipping the drink they had been provided with.

'I apologise for my behaviour earlier. You must think me very uncouth,' Ruth spoke quietly.

'Not at all. I was glad to see you free of your cage. You fly with complete confidence and grace.' He grinned at her, and she had to glance down at the fire to regain her own composure. 'Anyway, I think I must make amends to you.'

'No, you mustn't. There is nothing to be done.' Ruth glanced nervously around her. 'I think they plan to write to my father proposing a match for me, but without explaining who he may be.' She spoke very quietly, but was desperate to have him on her side.

'Calm yourself. I mean for compromising you twice over. If we had been seen in the church or in the woods, the gossips would have a field day. I propose to attend the assembly rooms at a time that is convenient, so that we may meet in more respectable circumstances. Remember, you must forget any other meeting.' He winked at her.

'I have written to my father. Could you possibly see that it gets to him?'

'Mr Molton, could we ... ' Mrs Fairley had walked briskly over to them, but she too was interrupted.

'Mr Upton, sir,' Stills announced from the door.

Samuel stood straight. Ruth noticed James glance to Samuel as the portly figure of Mr Upton walked briskly into the room with his arm resting dramatically in a sling, edged with silk and monogrammed 'A.T.T.'. Both men seemed to exchange unspoken words through their glance, and Ruth instantly suspected that there could be some connection between James and Samuel. But then, no, it was a fanciful notion. She needed to move away from her cousin's constant speculation; it was becoming a contagion.

'Robert, how well you look. What beauty surrounds us this evening — your lovely wife, her sister . . . ' He glanced at Mrs Fairly, who giggled, whilst James appeared to cringe slightly. ' . . . and the lovely Miss Grainger.' He walked over to Ruth. 'I am delighted to see you so recovered, and looking delightful.'

Robert and Mrs Fairly rejoined them.

'I am fine, Mr Upton; I trust your

arm is recovering well?' Ruth felt obliged to ask, but she displayed no genuine concern toward him, because he had abused her more by holding her as he had. His turn from coward to brave defender in the eyes of Eliza and Mrs Fairly made her angry. Yet she had to stifle any urge to show this, as she lived in their house and was dependent on their hospitality as her parents had wished.

'It pains me still, but I bear it well. It was a desperate act, but to save such a lovely young lady as yourself it was nothing — I would have accepted much worse a fate to see you safe, my dear.' He lifted his head up.

Ruth wanted to tell him what she really thought, but her situation was impossible without causing a great deal of insult to her guardian. She was dependent upon their goodwill and so she said nothing. Samuel was being careful to stand back a little.

'Excellent, Mr Upton,' said Mrs Fairly. 'See, Ruth's gratitude has left her lost for words. Well, sir, you escort Ruth into dinner and I'm sure your pain will be lessened.' She manoeuvred Ruth next to him.

James took Eliza's arm and Samuel followed with Robert as they walked along the narrow room that linked the drawing room with the dining room, being of a sufficient length to keep the sound from one room disturbing the activity in the other. This was particularly convenient when the ladies retired, leaving the men to their port.

Ruth tried not to look at Upton, who was seated at her side, but could not help but find comfort in the way Samuel had swapped places with James so that he sat opposite Ruth.

Robert, at the head of the table, continually brought Upton into the conversation or drew what detail he could from Samuel about his past. Ruth noticed his answers were all carefully worded to give little away, but he was a man of wealth.

Two hours later the meal was

finished and the women had retired to the drawing room. Ruth was tired and bored. She had listened to Eliza talk about the three eligible men at length, noting that she only linked Ruth's prospects to Upton or the mysterious Mr Molton, not James. When the men joined them it was Ruth who was encouraged to play the pianoforte first. Fortunately it was Samuel who turned the music for her, as she doubted if Upton knew how to.

The one highlight of the evening came to Ruth at the very last moment as the ladies prepared to retire, when Mrs Fairly turned to Samuel. 'Mr Molton, I trust your room meets your approval?'

'Indeed, ma'am.' He looked at Eliza and Ruth. 'Do the ladies ride? I always take my horse out in the mornings. Would you care to join me?' He looked to Robert.

'Oh, no, I'm afraid not. I cannot abide being upon an animal,' Eliza said, and made to leave. 'Perhaps Robert could join you?' she added.

'Unfortunately not. I have a business engagement with Mr Upton.'

'I enjoy riding and would be glad to join you, sir,' Ruth spoke up. She could not help but look at the surprised face of Mrs Fairly.

'Excellent idea! I shall ride over at eleven tomorrow and show you the area,' James's voice cut in. Mrs Fairly and Robert both smiled, and it was duly arranged. It was only Eliza and Upton whose faces showed little approval.

11

Ruth had been careful not to overeat at the dinner party, unlike Upton. She had also been watchful of the amount of wine she had drunk with the meal. Her playing and singing, thus unaffected, had been well received, but she had happily let the eager Eliza take over playing, whilst James turned the pages for her. In all, it had been a tolerable evening, but Ruth had longed for it to end to be rid of Upton's persistent attention. It was intrusive when she longed to be left to talk to Samuel. She had seen Upton staring at him on more than one occasion and was fretful that he too sensed some familiarity about him — or had he recognised him also?

Next morning, dressed in her riding outfit with a short military-style jacket, and carrying her long crop, Ruth made her way along the landing from her bedchamber to the top of the stairs.

Eliza's bedraggled figure emerged from her husband's room. She was wearing her floor-length dressing gown; her hair, unkempt and undone, fell loosely onto her shoulders. She looked pale without her make-up and very sleepy. Not the usual portrait of marital bliss that she repeatedly showed and professed to Ruth throughout the day.

'Good morning, Eliza,' Ruth said quietly, not wanting to wake Mrs Fairly, as she had hoped that she would be able to slip out before the ladies had woken for their hot chocolate drink. She had felt their disapproval the previous evening and had no wish to be prevented from escaping for a few hours from the suffocation of their company.

Eliza looked startled, but held her shoulders straight and walked over to her own bedchamber door. 'You are up and about indecently early, Ruth. For goodness' sake, take off that ridiculous outfit and have your rest.' Her words were snapped out harshly.

'Eliza, it is gone ten and I have an engagement to keep,' Ruth explained, when none should have been needed.

Eliza's eye had been focused on the door handle, which she had just turned. Ruth realised she had the effects of too much wine this morning playing with her head. Eliza stared blearily at Ruth and leaned over to her.

'Don't go making play for any other type of engagement, Ruth, because you are hunting in the wrong place.' Eliza forced a smile onto her face.

'I have no intention of doing any such thing.' Ruth could still smell the stale alcohol on Eliza's breath. 'But why would it be wrong?'

'Good, because James isn't interested in you. He does not care for bold women. And as for Mr Molton, he may well be a womaniser and opportunist, but my Robert will sort him out if he is. You, Miss Grainger, are spoken for; you are for Mr Upton!' The smile turned to a sneer. 'You will be his bride and settled soon enough.'

Ruth did not know whether to laugh or cry at the suggestion. It seemed so ludicrous. 'I am most definitely not, Eliza! I will decide for whom I am destined, when the time is right.' Ruth glared at her, knowing she should have just walked away and let the woman return to her slumber, but she had had far too much of Eliza's interference.

'That's what you think. Your father will give his permission and you will be Mrs Archibald Upton by winter!'

'Eliza, why are you so sure about this?' Ruth asked, stifling her anger behind her growing curiosity.

'Because Robert wills it so, and he is a man who always has what he wishes.'

Ruth laughed. 'Does he indeed? I shall see you at dinner, Eliza. Sleep well.' Ruth did not wait for a reply, but noticed how Eliza had paled still further at the mention of dinner. 'He does not own me as he does you, Eliza.' She saw her face look ashen and left her alone; there was no more to be said.

Entering the hall, Ruth had already had a tray brought to her room so she was ready and early for the agreed ride. Why, though, would Robert wish to see her wed to Upton? What on earth would he gain from it other than a companion for his young wife? Her father would never agree — she would see to that.

She waited for a servant to cross from the morning room to the servants' stairs and disappear from sight. Quickly, she slipped into Robert's study. The mahogany-lined room was dark and austere. A huge antlered head poked out from the wall over his desk, the glassy eyes of the hapless beast fixed in a piercing, unchangeable stare.

She sat down on the polished leather chair and remembered the times as a child when she had done the same on her father's. There she found the pen, ink and paper that she needed. Wasting no time, she began to write, making sure not to drip one single drop of ink on the desk papers. This letter had to be written and sent in secret.

Dear Father,

    I hope you are well and making good progress in the great battles you fight. I am so proud of you and Mama. Please send her my love and good wishes.

    I hate to burden you with extra worries, but I must ask for your patience and support in a very personal and troublesome matter . . .

She had no wish to explain every detail of what had happened, from the robbery onwards, but begged him not to agree under any circumstances to a match between her and a Mr Archibald Upton, no matter what her guardian wrote on the subject. His motives on this issue were with his friend and not with her. She trusted that her father would never doubt that she would act with the utmost propriety and never place herself in a situation whereby she would be forced into marrying such a man, against her and his wishes.

After sealing the letter with wax, she quickly put everything back in its place so as not to leave any evidence of what she had done. She looked at the desk drawer, listened to hear if anyone was about, and then slowly pulled it open. Guiltily she peeked within it, and was surprised to discover a pistol. There were papers also, and what seemed like a large amount of notes . . . bankers' notes. Quickly she closed the drawer and extinguished the lamp, hoping it would cool down before anyone saw it.

Once in the hallway, Ruth stepped onto the black-and-white chequered floor, holding the letter behind her back. She could hardly ask Robert to send it, for surely he might intercept it. Once the wax was dried she slipped it into her pocket.

'Miss Grainger, good morning.' She saw Samuel as he entered from the morning room where he had broken his fast.

In his single-breasted caped riding coat, he looked a fine figure, in Ruth's opinion. 'Good morning, Mr Molton.' She tried not to stare.

'If you are ready to go now, should we?' He gestured toward the outside.

'Yes.' Ruth walked to the large black painted doors and then glanced around them. 'Are we not going to wait for the lieutenant, Mr Molton?'

Samuel opened the door, looked at her with a slightly amused glint in his eyes, and smiled. 'He sent word that he had been unavoidably detained and asked us to proceed without him.' He winked cheekily at her, and she walked outside.

'Tell me honestly, Mr Molton, did this message arrive this morning or did he give you it yesterday evening?' Ruth asked, as the horses were brought around to them.

'No matter. We can enjoy our ride in peace without further interruption.' He glanced back at the house. 'Unless you prefer he was here?' he added in a thoughtful vein.

Once seated upon the horse she looked at him. 'It would be a shame for the horses not to have their promised exercise, I think.'

'I wholeheartedly agree.'

It was with a lightness of heart that Ruth walked her horse alongside Mr Molton's down the long driveway.

From an upstairs window a short, stout figure looked on. In slippers and nightshirt, with an aching arm and troubled heart, he watched the woman he desired ride out with the handsome stranger. A stranger who in some unfathomable way made him feel as though he should know him from somewhere — but where? Whoever Molton was, he had to be removed from Ruth's presence. The girl was showing far too much interest in him, and it was Upton himself she should be paying attention to. Somehow, he swore, he would be the undoing of Mr Samuel Molton. He wondered if he were a gambling man. The sooner he contrived a plan, the better. Perhaps he could relieve him of some of his obvious wealth.

12

'Where are we riding to?' Ruth asked as Samuel led her beyond Robert's land and onto a narrow track which led along the south of the dale, skirting the woods that covered the side.

'If we cut through the old forest track and take a sharp turn across the moor, I can show you something which will explain my presence here.' He turned the reins over in his hand thoughtfully. 'If I place my trust in you, will you let me down, Miss Ruth Grainger? Or can I trust you still further than I have already?'

Ruth thought for a moment, and saw her delay was concerning him. He doubted his judgement. Then she knew she could prove to him what he needed. 'Eliza has just told me that Robert wishes to make a match between myself and Upton. I have written this letter to send to my father, but have no safe means of sending it to him. Will you help me, sir? Can I trust you, Mr Samuel Molton? Or will you let me down?' She held out her letter to him and saw a look of satisfaction on his face as he extended his arm and took the letter from her, placing it carefully in his coat pocket.

'Then we are in accord,' he said. 'Together we shall defeat Upton's plans. We must make speed, though, as I do not wish to raise suspicion.'

Without further explanation, they galloped until they had approached a manor house which must have been built in the Jacobean period. Unlike the clean lines and angular symmetry of Robert's modern house, this building, to Ruth, had character and history to add to its charm. They neared the great wooden doors that were firmly closed. Ruth could see that its windows were shuttered. Its history had possibly been troubled of late, as it appeared to be closed up.

Samuel rode to the back of the house, where a small stable block was attached to a brick building — a small smithy, by the look of it. Another building had once been a laundry and dairy. He dismounted and walked his horse into an empty stall, then came out again for Ruth. He helped her to dismount. There was a mounting block, but instead of taking her over to it he held her waist and she slipped down the side of the animal to be steadied in his arms. He held her a moment or two longer than was strictly necessary.

'You can release me now, Samuel,' she said as he grinned at her.

'Forgive me; I let my thoughts take precedence over my manners.' He took a step back and led her horse into the stall next to his. When he reappeared he caught hold of her hand in his. 'Come, I shall show you the inside.'

He was walking her across the uneven flagstones to what would have been the kitchen. Releasing the catch from the side of the door, they entered the large stone space. The old spit and open fire were still and cold; ash-stained brick stood as testament to a very busy past. They told of many meals and feasts, and the activity of its previous existence.

'Surely, Samuel, we are trespassing. Who owns this place? Why are we here?' Ruth followed him along a narrow, worn corridor that led to two arched doorways. She stepped through one as Samuel entered the old hall by the other. A huge stone fireplace would once have warmed this fine place. Opposite, stone stairs led up to a wooden panelled gallery and the rooms and halls above. To the side of the main hall, two long oak tables had been stacked. Dust sheets covered the chairs, giving them an eerie, ghostly presence. Samuel walked over to the empty fire grate and placed one hand upon the carved stone surround. He looked thoughtfully down at the fire's empty chasm.

Ruth thought she understood, at least

in part. 'This was your home, wasn't it?' She walked over to him and placed her hand gently within his.

'It was my uncle's house. He took me in when my father was at sea. Mother would stay here. She played and sang, like you do.' He looked at her with sad eyes.

Ruth looked up at him, feeling a sudden empathy for him, because they had both been separated from their parents and left at the goodwill of relatives. She stroked his cheek with one gloved finger, tenderly, not really knowing why. It seemed a natural gesture. She wanted to comfort him and support him in whatever quest he was on. Justice, whatever it was, would be done.

He laughed and gave her a hug, swinging her around in the vast space before placing her feet back upon the stone floor. 'Ruth, you are so naive — beautiful both inside and out.' He lightly kissed her cheek, before releasing her and stepping back. 'How easy it would be to dupe you. Mr Upton shall not have you; it would be a travesty.' He looked away quickly and, regaining a more correct composure, continued. 'My mother sang and played abysmally, unlike you, who are very talented. She now lives in warmer climes and entertains my father each evening. He, who is nearly deaf through too many battles and cannons resounding in his ears, listens in contented glee. There is no sadness there other than the inevitable passage of time that no one can hold back. However, the anger and sadness that you so sensitively realised that I feel are due to my anger towards Mr Upton. He tricked my uncle out of the deeds for this lovely, ungainly place, and I sought to return them to the family. In time this will be his home once more, and then I shall inherit it when he no longer has need of the place.'

'So have you secured them? Have you righted the wrong?' Ruth asked, slightly annoyed that he could read her thoughts so easily, but touched that he did, and flattered by his comments.

'Yes, I have. They are beyond Upton's and my gullible uncle's grips once more. I had to break the law in order to bring justice in its place. My uncle was tricked, and Upton is no more than a thief.'

'So you stole them back.' She did not see a trace of regret in his face as he nodded.

'There is something more worrying behind all of this, Ruth. Robert appears to be deeply embroiled in Upton's business dealings . . . and that could affect you and your cousin Eliza. It will cast shadows upon the family if he too is breaking laws. It could even bring ruin upon them.' He gently placed his hand on her arm. 'Ruth, will you still help me if that is the price of justice?'

Ruth looked at his hand, liking the closeness, knowing it was too close, and fearing the question he had just asked. This man could destroy Eliza's dreams and life.

13

Robert sat down to a very late breakfast with Upton. He'd had the food served in his office and broken with his usual habit of eating in the dining room. He wanted to make sure they were not disturbed by his mother-in-law or Eliza.

'Bryant is not a happy man, Archibald. He wanted the manor house, we promised him it, and now he is angry and disappointed. This is not the best of starts to our growing enterprise. If he becomes difficult and gets drunk at the club, he could say too much to the wrong people. James is ever watchful; he dotes on Eliza. I wish he would be sent to Spain or the colonies.'

'I noticed she is quite taken by him,' Archibald said quietly.

'They can dote all they like. Childhood infatuation. But she is my wife! I will deal with James in time; for now he has his uses.' Robert stared at his plate and pushed his coddled egg unenthusiastically with his fork.

'I have an idea, Robert. We offer Bryant the choice of a horse from the stables for the next York meeting — any horse for three races. The winnings he can pocket as a gesture of good faith to smooth over his disappointment. I'll arrange a carriage, and your driver can act as his man for the day. What say you?' He belched as he gulped down a mug of hot chocolate, a treat he was particularly partial to.

'Yes, excellent! You are ingenious at times. The assembly room's opening dance is next week. He can join us there after his day out.' He paused. 'What if he loses? Won't it make things worse?' Robert looked worried.

'That is the nature of the sport. However, what he wins from the horse, he will lose on other issues — such as buying into our portfolio of colonial investments. He cannot lose on the horse, for I will have made arrangements for it to win.'

131

'Do we have a portfolio?' Robert looked surprised.

'No, but I am thinking of starting one if I can gather together enough investors to pay for a shipload of commodities.'

Robert shook his head. 'Do not diversify too far too soon, Archibald. We need to keep a firm hand on our business ventures. But don't you see? We buy one that is barely fit to sail, let it sink, and claim the insurance upon it.'

'I know a captain at Whitby who has an interest. I think we can do a deal . . . in time.' Upton's smile wavered. 'We have another issue that needs urgent attention, I feel.'

Robert raised an eyebrow, suspecting Upton's concern would be in some way connected with Ruth.

'Mr Molton. He appears to be captivating my intended. I don't care for him; neither do I trust him, Robert. There is something about the man which is familiar, yet I cannot place it. I am sure I have never been introduced to him before, or I would know his name. Miss Grainger appears to be comfortable in his presence, almost to the point of impropriety. I would ask you to intervene on my behalf as soon as you are able to.' Upton wiped the grease from his mouth on the starched napkin.

'I await a reply from her father,' Robert said. 'I have inferred that you and she have grown close and that she has acted rashly, so to prevent her and his family's good name being marred I have acted swiftly, and am having the banns read out in church next Sunday. It will be difficult to attend with enthusiasm the morning after the dance, but we shall. Should Ruth need to sleep in she will not hear them until the second reading the following week. I shall limit her freedom during this period. By the time we have her father's reply, you and she will be man and wife.' He grinned, pleased with his daring. 'She will have to agree, or face ruination.'

'Excellent — so we shall be married

within the month!' The man's eyes shone and he stood up. 'I must go to the tailor immediately.' He dropped the napkin on his empty plate and then paused. 'Ruth has not been overly encouraging to me, Robert, despite my flattery and the attention I have bestowed upon her.'

'Nor should she be. It would hardly be appropriate.' Robert leaned back in his chair.

'No, no of course not! However, she will be conducive to this arrangement, won't she? I do not expect her enthusiasm, but I need her complicity. Her dissent would be difficult to excuse.'

'Archibald, at the assembly rooms you shall make sure you and she have a moment alone. I shall see to it that you are seen together — alone. You will embrace her. Her name will be scandalised should you not become engaged and save her reputation. We shall slip something into her punch. Her wits will be dulled. Before she realises her impropriety it will be too late. You are to be her saviour from ruination. I will see to it that she is shamed into this match, and she will listen to me because, by my letting her have a modicum of freedom with Molton, she has no suspicion that it is you whom I wish her to wed. She will think I am still acting in her own best interests.

'So settle yourself, man. You will make sure that you go far enough with her to make your match a must, but not enough to harm her reputation irrevocably. Once she has been seen with you, then you can do what you will behind closed doors. Now, find out what you can about the new man Molton. What is his weakness: women, gambling, drink, opium, or greed? He will have one; and when you find it, then we shall have him.'

14

Ruth and Samuel remounted and rode back along the drive. Samuel dismounted, being careful to close the ornate iron gates behind them and refasten the chain. It was as he had placed the key to the lock within his pocket that he was aware of another rider approaching. He quickly took hold of the reins of his horse from Ruth and looked at her reassuringly, as she had instantly looked guilty.

'Good day, sir,' Samuel said loudly. The rider looked quite sternly at both of them. Then, almost as if he had just remembered his manners, he removed his riding hat, revealing a head of silver-grey hair, neatly cut, and acknowledged Ruth's presence before replacing it in a grand fashion. He raised the silver-topped cane in his hand and addressed Samuel directly.

'Yes, and good day to you, too. Tell

me, sir, do you own this property?'

'We were passing. I thought it looked an interesting but neglected place, and am in the market for a new estate.' Samuel remounted his horse, watching the stranger curiously.

'Damnation!' the man exclaimed.

Ruth looked away. She wanted to laugh, but bit her lip as it would be as improper as his comment for her to do so.

'I apologise, miss. It's just the frustration of it all.' He appeared to Ruth to be genuinely flustered.

'Whatever is the matter, sir?' Samuel asked politely. Ruth sensed he was brimming with curiosity and she wondered if they had stumbled across one of Mr Upton's associates.

'I so wanted to purchase this house. I had the funds organised and was about to do the deal when the deeds went missing. Damned bad luck, eh? I tell you, this place would suit me fine. But can I find out who holds the deeds? Can I? No, or I'll be bu — ' He glanced at Ruth, letting out a long sigh. 'No, I can't!'

'Why is it so important to you? Surely there are other properties in the area. I believe there are new, quite grand houses being built around Gorebeck — quite fashionable by all accounts. Would they not interest you?' Samuel asked.

'By the gods, man! Do I look like a man of fashion? I'm not a dandy or a fop, sir. Fashion . . . humbug! No, they would not suit me. You cannot build history! This . . . ' He pointed to the building with his cane. 'This is a part of our heritage. We should protect it, not let it stand ruinous! It should be owned by a worthy man, and I am that man. I jolly well respect it for what it is.'

'Perhaps, sir, if you would care to give me your card, I may enquire as to who owns it. I shall be pleased to contact you should my enquiries be fruitful, and if I find that the owner wishes to sell it.'

'You and your young lady are not thinking of living here, are you? I mean, damned draughty places, miss. I'm sure the two of you would be cosier in one of the 'fashionable' residences.'

Ruth blushed and looked away.

'No, sir. We were merely riding when we happened across it. I have always admired such places. We have no plans to buy a home . . . yet.' Samuel glanced at her, a smile on his face as he added the last presumptuous word.

'Good, good.' The man sounded relieved.

'Your card, sir,' Samuel repeated.

'Yes, yes of course.' He opened a silver card case and fumbled with gloved fingers to slide one out, then presented it to Samuel.

'Thank you.' Samuel read the embossed writing on the card. 'Mr Bryant, I am Mr Samuel Molton, recently arrived from London. I shall be in contact with you when I have made further enquiries.'

'Good man. I shall not be ungrateful for your efforts.'

'There will be no need for that, but please tell me — if you had funds arranged, with whom had you made the arrangements to buy the property?'

Mr Bryant looked at Samuel and for once did not speak without thought. 'Oh, a business associate; it is of little import, as he has not been able to provide the deeds.' He winked at Samuel, nodded to Ruth and then rode off.

'What a peculiar man,' Ruth exclaimed.

'Indeed, but now we know whom Upton was stealing the documents for. There has to be a connection via Upton and Robert.'

'What will you do, Samuel?' Ruth asked as he placed the card in his inside pocket.

'Make enquiries, as I promised.' He gestured that they should walk on.

'But you already know who owns it.' Ruth wondered what game he played.

'Ah, but they are not the enquiries that I am going to make.'

He watched as she could not help herself from showing her concern. 'You could be placing yourself in a great deal of danger. Why not talk to the lieutenant? Surely he could help.'

'James will no doubt do what he can.'

Ruth stopped her horse and Samuel looked back at her. 'What is it?'

'You two know each other, don't you? That is why he spoke out last night, making this morning's ride possible.'

He walked his horse back to her so that they were facing each other. 'We were at school together. We have been lifelong friends, Ruth . . . and you are far too observant for a young maid.'

'The more I learn of you, sir, the more complex my life is becoming.' She flushed and looked up at him, shocked. 'If James is aware of you and your doings, then he knows that I lied about the highwayman!' With wide eyes she saw a grim expression cross his face and was filled with a sense of shame and foreboding. 'What will he think of me? What a fool I've been!' Ruth was going to turn her horse away but he leaned over, placing his hand upon hers.

'Don't feel so bad. You did, without realising it, help us in our pursuit of justice. Your motives do not concern him.' He lowered his head to hers, looking into her eyes. 'I want to keep you safe, Miss Grainger. I do not want Upton anywhere near you. When you are at the dance I shall be watching you closely. Do not leave yourself in a situation where you can be separated from the main throng of people. I shall be there.' He kissed her cheek and, despite her best resolve, she lifted her lips to his and savoured the intimacy that followed.

'We must return,' Ruth said, after having reluctantly parted from his tender caress.

'We shall.' But before they did, he held her reins firmly in his hand. 'Ruth, what Robert wants and what he has coming to him are two very different outcomes. Eliza must be none the wiser. James will take care of her when justice is served.'

Ruth looked at the man, her stranger, and nodded her acceptance and agreement. She was committed to a path but had no idea where it would lead.

She held out her letter. 'You will see that it is sent?'

He nodded, and she trusted him with all her heart.

* * *

Upton left the office, buoyed up by the news that he would soon be a respectably married man. His future was almost secure . . . almost. He was so preoccupied with pulling his gloves onto his stubby fingers, eager to take the coach back to his office, that he nearly walked into Mrs Fairly as she stepped off the stairs into the hallway.

'My good lady, I do apologise.' He supported her elbow as she regained her balance. Her lace cap swayed at the side of her face in a pendulum motion.

'You are in a hurry this morning, sir. I take it you have not had bad news?' She stepped discreetly backwards.

'No, the opposite would be the case. I had a divine evening yesterday, and am heartily looking forward to joining you at the ball on Saturday.' He placed his hat upon his head.

'Yes, Eliza is very excited by it. However, I did not think you enjoyed the crowded dance hall.' Mrs Fairly remembered how the previous season he had become so hot and uncomfortable that he had taken to leaving the room to breathe fresh air.

'Oh, I was under the weather last season, but this year I am in fine form . . . my peak, you might say.'

Mrs Fairly thought she might not. 'What of your injured arm?'

'I have braved it for Miss Grainger's safety. Now, it only pains me when I think how near to danger that poor lady fell, and your own good self. However, soon she will help me to mend in every way.'

Mrs Fairly was tempted to use the sharpness of her tongue to cut him to the quick, but decided to say nothing.

'You must excuse me, as I have much to do in a short time.' He bowed with a flourish, which served nothing but to

144

emphasise his portly figure.

'You must be on your way then. Do not let me detain you further. Has the driver been summoned?'

He smiled in a way that Mrs Fairly did not care for. 'Yes, he is serving me for a few days. He has the carriage outside.'

'He is a reliable driver; you are in good hands, sir,' Mrs Fairly added.

'Indeed!' he said, and flounced out.

Mrs Fairly looked at Robert, who had just appeared from the library. 'Robert, is Mr Upton well? He appears very distracted this morning.'

'He is a happy man, that is all. Mrs Fairly, when James returns from his ride, will you ask him to see me? I shall be in the library.' He went to walk into the room.

'Morning, Robert.' A bleary-eyed Eliza descended the stairs.

Robert glanced at her. 'Morning, my dear.' He smiled at her as she struggled to respond in kind.

'Excuse me, sir,' his butler spoke out,

'The lieutenant did not go out riding this morning. I believe that Mr Molton had received a message to say he was unavoidably detained.'

Eliza's head shot up; she winced. 'Does this mean that Ruth has gone riding with Mr Molton alone? The gossip will be too much. What possessed her?'

Robert dismissed the servant. 'Indeed, it does. Mrs Fairly, this is not acceptable. It leaves her open to speculation and gossip. I shall occupy more of Mr Molton's time and I would strongly advise that you two do the same of Ruth. She must be prepared for the ball, and I will hold you both responsible should she not be turned out respectably and with her good character beyond reproach. She has acted very naively, and needs more guidance.'

'We shall certainly do our best,' replied Mrs Fairly.

'We will guarantee it, Robert!' Eliza said, for once glaring at her mother and taking the upper hand.

Robert stormed upstairs. 'Have my

horse made ready. I must go to town.'

Eliza took hold of her mother's hand and led her into the morning room. She sent the maid to deliver Robert's order to the stable lad and then to fetch them sweet tea. She then sat her mother down in the chair opposite her own by the large mantelpiece.

'Mama, I have something to share with you, but you must be the soul of discretion.' She leaned forward, still holding the older woman's hand.

'I am always discreet, Eliza.' Sternly, she watched her daughter as the younger woman glanced back at the door to make sure that it was safe to pass on her latest piece of gossip.

'It is concerning Ruth. She is to wed Mr Upton!' Eliza raised her eyebrows and sat back, relieved of her burden of secrecy.

'Is she? Does she know this yet?' Mrs Fairly asked, thinking that she already knew the answer before she asked, as she had heard every word of the conversation in Robert's office. In her life she had learned that it often paid to listen to such private assignations.

'Well, she should not know but . . . she may.' Eliza looked guiltily down at her hands.

'You told her what Robert intends!' Mrs Fairly shook her head, wondering what farce was about to unfold in her household. She was sure Robert had not told her gullible daughter the depth of his and Upton's plans.

'Only that Robert wants her to marry his friend . . . for her own good.' Eliza looked up, justifying her actions as best as she could.

Mrs Fairly looked at her. 'How did Ruth react?' She realised that Eliza had unwittingly revealed to Ruth Robert's whole intention. Ruth was not like Eliza, malleable and driven by the desire for trinkets, position and possessions. She was headstrong and would not easily bend to Robert's or anyone's will if it clashed with her own. Upton was the last person Ruth would consider for a husband after the way he had grabbed her during the robbery.

'I don't think she took it very seriously, but she should. Mr Upton has a growing fortune and a good name in the community.' Eliza looked indignantly at her mother.

'Eliza, say no more of this to either Ruth or Robert. Let it rest. I'm sure he knows what is best. We shall merely prepare for the ball.' Mrs Fairly smiled as instantly her daughter's face lit up with joy, all else forgotten by her, but not by Mrs Fairly.

15

A dry evening was prayed for and granted to the affluent families of the region. Eliza was resplendent in a lime-green gossamer satin dress, with matching emerald necklace. Tiny yellow silk flowers edged the neckline and the rich Italian crêpe train, with tight sleeves finished with Belgian lace. Eliza held her head high which, with the jewelled feather head apparel, contrasted with her dark brown hair and accentuated her tall, thin figure.

Mrs Fairly had chosen a simpler style in rich maroon velvet, showing a skirt of fine cream silk, while upon her head was a turban, bejewelled and edged in gold. For a lady who normally dressed quite plainly in her day wear, she cut a respectable and fashionable figure.

Ruth had reluctantly agreed to show some enthusiasm for the evening and had been lavished with an ivory silk gown overlaid with the finest lace and edged around the neckline with small pearls. She had been uncomfortable with the scoop of the neckline at first and a compromise had been reached by adding a little Paris net, although she was still aware that it showed plenty of her curvaceous shape, as Mrs Fairly had explained, to its best advantage. With a contrasting azure crêpe shawl, she was relieved to see that her hair would be adorned with only a simple fine band of pearls. She almost felt like a bride, rather than a lady dressed for a ball.

Eliza's ceaseless excitement and enthusiasm had been contagious and it was with some high spirits that Ruth eventually arrived. Her only sadness was that, after her ride with Samuel that blissful morning, she had been prevented from openly having any opportunity to speak to him alone, even though they were guests under the same roof. It had been frustrating for both of them, as they occasionally looked longingly at each other — discreetly, she hoped — each evening as Eliza played endless tunes on the pianoforte.

The night before the ball, though, Ruth had returned to her room to find Samuel waiting for her. She had nearly screamed because, as he had heard her enter, he had hidden behind the long, heavy curtains, and when they moved as he stepped out he had given her quite a fright.

Fortunately, his whisper stopped her. 'It's me, Ruth. Samuel.'

'What are you doing in my bedchamber?' She looked back at the closed door, fearing they would be heard.

'I had to speak with you alone before tomorrow evening.' He had walked over to her, looking most concerned. 'Please do not be alarmed.'

'I am not alarmed,' she maintained.

'No.' He smiled at her, and kissed her quickly and lightly on her lips.

She wished he had lingered longer, and knew she should be ashamed for having such thoughts, but the truth was that she wasn't in the least. 'Perhaps a little bit, but so I should be. If you were caught in here . . . '

'They would usher me out of the house. Nothing would be made of it, because they would not want your reputation sullied before your engagement is announced at the ball to Mr Upton.' He stared at her as if judging her response.

'Preposterous! I will leave here this night. Have you come to rescue me?' Her voice sounded hopeful. She placed her hand on his arm.

'I shall rescue you, but not like that. We shall not opt for elopement. I intend to beat Mr Upton and Robert at their own game. But first, before I bring upon us the consequence of my actions, I need to ask you something.'

'Samuel, you talk in riddles. What consequences? What actions? What game are they playing?' Ruth was pleased that he circled her with his arms. She felt safe; loved, even. Yet, knowing this was the most dangerous situation for a girl's reputation, she still felt foolishly drawn into wanting this man to love her and to trust him.

'Mr Upton is to compromise you at the ball, so I have been informed, and you shall be forced by circumstance into an engagement.' He leaned his forehead against hers.

'That will not happen,' she replied.

'I know, because if you are agreeable, I shall compromise you first.'

Ruth giggled, then regained her composure and stepped back. 'This cannot be. What will my father make of it?'

'I intend that we announce our engagement. There will be so many people present it will not be easily rebuffed. Whilst we are in this arrangement, your letter, accompanied with my own, will make their way to your father. You will be at liberty to withdraw from the engagement, but of course I will not be able to without causing myself a deal of financial loss and you a damaged reputation. I therefore need to know, Ruth, how the idea sits with you?' He stood before her. 'Honestly, I have a reputable past. I served in the war and resigned my commission after being held for a time by the French. My father was a magistrate, my mother a bishop's daughter.'

'Oh stop it, Samuel. Save it for my father. I care not who your parents are, only that I care for you, and . . . ' He smiled and Ruth looked away, seeing her bed. She blushed and looked the other way.

Samuel stifled a laugh and patted her shoulder. 'Then I have my answer, and I shall see you at the ball. Do not venture on your own unless you receive a message which is followed by, 'If you so please, Miss Grainger.'

'Very well, but Samuel . . . you will take care.' She placed a hand on his arm.

'Yes, I will.' He leaned in to her and kissed her cheek. Her lips found his but he pulled away with a reluctant look. 'I must leave. Tell me one more thing, Ruth: would you want to build a nest, or would you care to travel with your husband first?'

'I think to travel would be a great adventure.'

'Good. My choice, too.' He went back to the window and opened it.

'What are you doing? Use the door!' Ruth was trying to keep her voice low.

'Too risky. If we are found here they would cover it up, lock you in until a forced marriage could be arranged, and as for me . . . well, I shall climb down here. We have our plan. Sleep well.' He disappeared from view.

Ruth peered over her small balcony and saw him land and roll on the ground below. He stood up, bowed and disappeared into the shadows.

A tap on the door made her jump. The maid entered and looked at her in horror. 'Miss, you'll catch your death of cold.' She shut the window firmly and drew the curtains back to their original position.

Sedan chairs were carried to the open entrance of the assembly rooms. Coaches and hackneys lined up along the street approaching the Corinthian pillars that adorned the building's classical frontage. Ladies were carefully aided into the building so their silk slippers did not touch the dirty ground outside.

The young went with eager hearts hoping to fix a match, an interest their parents would approve of and a marriage which would be conducive, if not one of love. The married and the disheartened went to see what tittle-tattle they could pick up and share with their friends and associates. Here fortunes were cemented or, at the gambling table in the gaming room, possibly lost.

Once the good people of society had been carefully deposited, the drivers and carriers descended the stairs to the basement. Their vehicles were safely parked behind the rooms. Here they were to spend the long evening playing cards, throwing dice, telling bawdy jokes and drinking a little until their services were required once more.

The driver was dismissed by Upton, at last, and was glad of a few hours to himself. He hated the cowardly man who had hidden behind a young girl's skirt. He had been with Mrs Fairly for years and could tolerate Mr Robert, but found being at Upton's beck and call very difficult. Why Mr Robert had decided he should work for the man, he did not know, but sincerely hoped it was no more than a temporary arrangement.

The driver was nudged; he turned and saw an extended hand holding a tankard to him. His throat was dry and the room, which held no ventilation, was already hot. He'd been offered a much-needed drink and so he took it. 'Cheers!' he shouted, but the hand was gone, so he sat on a stool watching a man lose his night's takings in a game of chance. That was before the fool had even earned it. He shook his head. It would not be that way for him. He had a lovely wife, Becky, and son to rear. The money he earned paid for their keep; any extra he saved for the lad. He'd have a life of his own, at no man's whim. So he sipped his drink, not paying attention to the man who had supplied him with it, but glad that it was free and decent. It was therefore quite a shock to him when his body suddenly felt very heavy and he slipped off the stool.

A strong arm linked under his and helped him back up. 'Come on, man — you're not even halfway through the night. You'll need to be sober to take them home.' He heard laughter, but could not focus. The room seemed blurred. What was happening to him? He couldn't be drunk; he'd had no more than a couple of gulps. He must be ill. He tried to speak, but his words were unclear.

'I need you. Where are you, man?'

Someone was summoning him. Upton, it was Upton. Why would he be down in the basement? It was no place for a gentleman, even Upton. Then he heard the voice rise . . . It *was* Upton. What was he doing down here, with working folk?

'My God, man, have you no shame? The man's a thief! I trusted you. We all trusted you. Wait till Robert hears of this, and poor Miss Grainger! I'll have this brooch restored to its rightful owner this evening. James, can you have him clapped in irons? You should have thought of the consequences. You have a family, man. It will be the workhouse for them.'

Arms pulled — no, dragged him to his feet. He felt the edge of the stairs on his shins as he was taken back up to the door, then a blast of cold air, and he realised he was outside again. The people had gone. They were having their ball. He saw two soldiers approaching. They held him, and he felt as though he were having a nightmare. He looked at the lieutenant, his head clearing slightly. 'Sir, what happened? I don't understand. I was having a drink and then my head swam.'

'Mr Upton found you drunk in the basement. Miss Grainger's brooch fell from your pocket. Did you aim to gamble it?' James's face was almost clear to him. The driver could see that the man looked concerned.

'Sir, you know me to be of good character. I did not . . . ' He shook his head. 'I only had one drink . . . I can't be drunk . . . I'm not a thief. Please tell Miss Grainger I didn't take it. That bastard did . . . ' He had no chance to finish his words. The soldiers took him off to the lock up, to wait for judgement by the magistrate. Stealing a gold brooch could get him hung or transported. As he was flung into the cell, he screamed out pitifully as he pictured his lovely wife and his only son.

16

The grand ballroom, despite being vast in size, heaved with over three hundred people within it. The main dance area was free until the music started, then partners were escorted onto the dance floor and the country dances began the proceedings, a light touch of the hand being allowed between men and women.

Mrs Fairly found some associates seated near the entrance. She joined them with, Ruth noted, a clear view of the entrance. Eliza and Robert took to the floor, but before Ruth could seat herself she saw Mr Upton approaching. He had an unnaturally bright smile on his face. In fact, she had never seen him appear so pleased with himself. Somehow his happiness only served to make her feel anxious. It was with a huge sense of relief that a hand took hold of hers. She looked up half-expecting to see Samuel, but instead she saw the jacket of a military man, and to her surprise it was James who escorted her swiftly away, following after Eliza and Robert onto the floor.

'I hope you don't mind my claiming the first dance, Miss Grainger,' he said quietly, as they faced one another.

'Not at all, sir. I am quite pleased.' She smiled at him and was relieved how much she enjoyed dancing under the large crystal chandeliers.

Once the dance ended, Mr Upton walked over to them. Before he could speak, James addressed him. 'Mr Upton, I should like to speak to you about the incident downstairs.'

'Here is hardly the time or the place, man.' Anxiously, he looked to Ruth and began to speak, but a very vocal Samuel interrupted.

'Ruth . . . Miss Grainger, how truly marvellous you look.' This time it was he who took her hand, and once again she found herself being escorted back to the dance floor. However, Samuel walked her to the other side of the room, whilst James placed an arm on Upton's shoulder and steered him into the gaming room.

Ruth glanced over her shoulder and saw that Robert was taking notice of everything that was happening. 'Samuel, we shall not be able to keep this up all evening,' she whispered into his ear as they came close.

'True, but then again we shall not have to.'

She looked at him curiously as she parted from him for a turn and a few steps on her own.

'Don't worry, just follow my lead . . .' The dance played on.

Robert tapped Upton on the shoulder. 'Excuse me, James. I have need of Mr Upton — business, you understand.' He was about to turn and take the man away from the table where James had seated them whilst he asked more detailed questions about what had happened in the basement. He knew the truth of it, but was merely occupying the man, whilst quietly fuming that a good man now lay, mortally crushed, within his cell.

James glared at Robert.

'Oh, what business could you have in here, James?' Robert was clearly curious as Upton stood and was eager to move away.

'Nothing of great import, Robert. Come, let us carry on with the dancing. I must attract Miss Grainger's attention.' Upton looked pointedly at Robert, who was about to do his bidding, but James's words stopped him in mid-step.

'I would have thought the arrest of your man, the driver, would be of interest to you, Robert.' James also stood.

'What do you mean, arrest? It cannot be possible. Whatever for?' Robert was visibly shocked.

'I did not want to mention it here,' said Upton. 'The man had Miss Grainger's stolen brooch upon his person. It fell to the floor when they were gambling down in the basement, and the man had been drinking . . . He was quite worse for wear!' He looked at Robert, whose eyes stared in disbelief.

'But he doesn't drink . . . hardly at all. His family are practically teetotal; they follow the Bible Moths. This is not like him. And why would he steal a girl's brooch when he has access to my house and has had my trust these past fifteen years?' His eyes searched James's face for an explanation, but the man shrugged his shoulders.

'I don't understand it either, but Mr Upton saw the brooch fall from the man's pocket. I had no choice but to arrest him.' James sighed. 'I am shocked myself. He has always shown integrity.'

Mr Upton looked at the two, his colour high. 'That is as may be, but his type can never be trusted. Their moral fibre will always succumb to temptation. Now, Robert, we should return.'

Robert stood straight. 'I'll deal with this later. Excuse us, James. We have business to discuss. Make sure he is treated well.'

James nodded and watched the two return to the crowded dance hall. A

166

fiery exchange appeared to take place between them, but it was short-lived as Mrs Fairly walked to join them. She tipped her fan slightly in James's direction and he nodded discreetly in return. Placing his glass upon the table, he exited via the doors onto the porch.

17

Eliza was beginning to wish that she had not chosen the dress pattern with the tight sleeves. The room was becoming stuffy and she felt hot and bothered. Worse still, Robert had disappeared with Mr Upton, James had vanished from sight, and her mother had slipped away while Eliza was dancing. Only Ruth was in sight, and she was behaving furtively with the mysterious Mr Molton. Then the unthinkable happened: the orchestra started to play a waltz. Most of the decent folk walked to the sides of the room. Mothers and fathers of unattached young women guarded their daughters, or escorted them out of the main dance hall so they should be spared the spectacle. This dance was a foreign import, which allowed far more contact than was acceptable between the sexes.

Ruth saw Mr Upton and Robert

enter from the gaming room. Eliza immediately showed her pleasure at seeing them as openly as she had shown her disparagement of the waltz.

'Robert, how uncomfortably crowded it is in here.' She smiled up at him. 'Should we take some fresh air in the garden?'

He grunted an acknowledgement to her, but did not answer or give any indication that he intended to take her up on the suggestion. Instead, he appeared to be looking for someone . . . Ruth!

'There, Upton, now is your chance. Move in quickly.' He gestured to where Ruth was standing with Samuel by the open doors that led onto the patio gardens to the rear of the building.

Before either man could move, Samuel swung Ruth onto the dance floor and, with some of the more daring engaged or married couples, they too danced. Ruth knew how to do the waltz, as she had watched in awe at previous balls; but she also knew that tongues would wag as she was with a single young man, herself unattached. So she smiled and looked into his eyes as they moved around the room.

Mrs Fairly took hold of Eliza's arm and walked her briskly over to Miss Connelly and her friends, immediately engaging in conversation while an irate Mr Upton looked on. 'Robert, this is no good. No good at all!' he said. 'We will have to stop him the moment the orchestra plays the last note, before her reputation is marred irreparably.'

Robert nodded. 'I shall intervene and then, man, you can tell me what on earth possessed you to have my driver arrested.'

'I believe he knows who the man is who stole those deeds. Once he has had a night in the cells, I'm sure he will feel more inclined to share that information with us. After all, if he does not, his wife will be left to find her own way of providing for their son, and I shouldn't think a man as proud as he could bear that.' Upton's lip curled.

Robert considered what he had said.

'You are a resourceful man, Archibald.'

The shorter man chuckled. 'Remember what I said: trust Upton!'

'Very well. Ah, the music is drawing to an end. Now step in there and rescue the little fool from that womaniser before I have her father's wrath at my door, screaming at me for the ruination of his precious daughter.'

The music finished and Upton let not a second pass before he almost ran over to Ruth. 'Miss Grainger, people are watching you. Please allow me to escort you for a lime cordial.' He turned to Mr Molton and stood as tall as he could. 'Sir, you should consider a young lady's reputation.' He tried to steer Ruth away, but, as the floor cleared, Ruth hesitated.

'Thank you, Samuel, for an excellent and memorable dance.' She smiled at him in a flirtatious manner, and felt Upton tense at her side.

Samuel bowed and winked at her, as she was walked away in front of disapproving eyes.

* * ★

'Sam, we have a problem.' James walked over to him as he collected a drink from a waiter and watched where Upton and Ruth were standing.

'Another one?' Samuel said, without taking his eyes off Ruth.

'Yes. Upton has accused Robert's driver of stealing Ruth's brooch. The man's desperate and he knows who you are and what you did. He saw you ride and recognised you instantly. He came to me, troubled, because he distrusts Upton and knows he is always making shady assignations with the likes of your Bryant fellow, but he has no such feelings about you. Fortunately it was I he approached and not Robert. Normally he would not say anything as per my recommendation and word that I shall look into the matter, but he has a family to care for. If they are threatened he will do what they want. I don't want to arrest you.' James paused.

'You will not have to, because you

have a description from Miss Grainger, and the driver has just been discredited. It would not stand before a magistrate, but it would destroy the man, and that I would not see done. We will find a solution, James, as always.' Samuel could see that his friend's attention was split. He was staring at Eliza.

James spoke quietly, 'She deserves better.'

'She deserves you,' Samuel replied.

'James, break up their union — say Ruth needs Eliza's help for a moment and then pass word to Mrs Fairly that I think ten will be a good time. She will know what to do.'

★ ★ ★

'Miss Grainger . . . Ruth. I should like to talk to you in private,' said Upton. 'There is an issue concerning your future and your parents that is most pressing. Should we take the air where I can speak openly, away from prying eyes and curious ears?'

173

'My parents, you say?' Ruth realised she was being lured into his trap, but the mention of her parents made her curious as to what he was prepared to say to gain her trust and interest.

He patted her arm. 'Not here. Let us slip out discreetly.' He pointed to the patio doors.

She glanced around and saw Robert. He lifted a glass to her and smiled approvingly. Ruth looked around for Samuel or James, as she slowly walked around the room with Upton. She was aware that she was being watched still, and wondered if her antics with Samuel would in the end help Upton's own plan. She had no intention of stepping anywhere with the man unchaperoned. If she did not do that, she could not be seen. James was talking to Mrs Fairly, Samuel was not there, but Eliza was approaching. Upton saw her and tried to make Ruth speed up, but she smiled and acknowledged Eliza.

'Honestly, Ruth, you acted disgracefully.' Eliza's outburst was for her and

Upton's ears only. She looked hot and uncomfortable.

'Pardon, Eliza, but I don't know what you mean. I have been enjoying myself, as you yourself said I would.' She paused and linked arms with her. 'You look hot, dear. Why don't you take a turn in the garden with Mr Upton? He was wanting to have some fresh air.' She looked at the man, whose face had flushed. 'Would you, sir? Then when Eliza is refreshed we shall be able to have our talk.'

Appeased by her last statement, Upton agreed and walked out into the mild evening air with Eliza.

Ruth, meanwhile, skirted the room looking for Samuel. It was Mrs Fairly who found her first. 'Ruth, that horrid man has had our driver arrested for stealing your brooch. He must have had it all the time. We must find a way to help him!'

'I shall speak for him,' Ruth said, and held Mrs Fairly's hand.

'Good. He has been a good driver,

servant and husband for many years. So now I must help you out of one mess and into another. I hope you know what you are doing with your life. Before you speak to James about him, Mr Molton wishes to have a private word with you in the library. It is the door down there, opposite the gaming room doors.'

'Thank you, Mrs Fairly,' Ruth added.

The older woman shook her head. 'Don't thank me yet. This game of charades may have far-reaching consequences that you cannot begin to imagine.'

18

Ruth approached James before she went anywhere else. He was speaking to the man who she recognised as Mr Bryant, from her ride with Samuel.

'Lieutenant, I must apologise for interrupting. However, there has been the most grievous mistake made and I fear it must be corrected as soon as possible.' Both gentlemen looked at her with great interest. Initially she had thought Mr Bryant had shown annoyance that his conversation had been cut in upon.

'Whatever is the matter, Miss Grainger?' James asked.

'You have arrested an innocent man. Our driver did not steal my brooch.' She thought she saw a look of relief cross James's eyes.

'Mr Upton saw it fall from his pocket. How could you explain this if he is, as you say, innocent? When I asked you to produce the brooch after the robbery you could not, and Mr Upton had seen that it had been stolen.' James shrugged his shoulders. 'I do not see how you can say he is innocent.' Although his words sounded dismissive, his face showed that he was willing for her to provide the solution to the driver's predicament.

'You are quite correct, but it was my mistake. I had put it safe in a pocket, and in the confusion forgotten where it was. Later, in gratitude for his bravery in our moment of need, I gave it to him as a gift. Merely as a token of my good-will, for his wife.' She looked down sheepishly. 'I apologise. I never thought that it would cause trouble, and in fact the gesture may have been a little inappropriate and rash. You must understand, though, I had been through a very frightening ordeal.'

'The scoundrel was about to gamble it on a game of chance!' Mr Bryant exclaimed loudly.

'On the contrary, he told me he would always keep it on him as a good-luck charm; he is a man of superstitious nature.' She saw James smile.

'It didn't work, did it?' Bryant laughed.

'I shall send word at once for him to be released,' said James. 'Thank you, Miss Grainger, for speaking up for the man. The consequences otherwise would have been dire.'

'It was the least I could do.' She glanced toward the library. 'If you would excuse me.' She left them.

★ ★ ★

Ruth tried not to be seen entering the library, and slipped inside once a crowd had passed her as the dance floor filled up again for the quadrille. It was so quiet. She saw a figure move quickly away from the open fire. Samuel strode over to her; oil lamps created a semi-flickering gloom, shrouding them.

'I thought that you had changed your mind and were happy to take your chance with Upton.' He pulled her gently towards him, but she could see that he was teasing her.

'That I would never do. Do you know he even tried to have our driver, the innocent man, locked up?' Ruth was disgusted with the man.

'Yes, it is an issue I have yet to resolve. He realised who I was.' Samuel sat on the two-seater settee that was placed cosily by the fire; he waited whilst Ruth sat next to him.

'I have already resolved it. There cannot have been a theft of an item that was freely given to the man, can there?' Ruth was very pleased at her quick thinking.

'Excellent. So now we have to solve your difficult circumstance.' He leaned towards her and cupped her face in his hand.

Ruth did not know what he had in mind, but one little innocent kiss would be enough to seal their fate should someone find them. Ruth lifted her lips to his willingly. She had had one eye watching the doors, but was completely unprepared for the eruption of emotions and feelings that swept through her as Samuel took an innocent kiss to a more intimate embrace. Ruth discovered what was meant by the sin of passion, as her feelings towards Samuel intensified with his touch. All thought of watching the door vanished from her mind. It was only when Samuel stood up abruptly and moved in front of her in a protective manner that she became aware that a group of people had entered the library too.

'Mrs Fairly, I . . . We were . . . ' Samuel began to speak in his normally confident manner, but each time he broke off, apparently at a loss for words.

'I can see well enough, sir, what you were about! How dare you, when we have had you under our roof, as our guest! And as for you, young lady . . . ' Behind Mrs Fairly stood James, Eliza, Robert, and Miss Connelly.

James stood forward. He had closed the doors behind him. 'Mr Molton, have you anything to say in your defence?'

'Indeed I have. I have asked Miss Grainger to be my wife and she has accepted.' Ruth stood at his side and slipped her hand into his.

Miss Connelly supported Mrs Fairly while taking everything in with great relish, her eyes wide with anticipation.

Robert stood forward, red-faced. 'I shall not allow it. This is preposterous! You shall not wed this girl. She is an innocent led astray. If your father were here, he would call you out, sir!'

'I doubt that, since duelling would be against Wesley's orders,' Samuel replied.

'Nevertheless, you have a ward with a damaged reputation, sir,' Miss Connelly spoke out.

'Not at all, madam,' said Samuel. 'I have already written to Miss Grainger's father expressing our desire to be wed, accompanied by references from my old colonel in chief, and an archdeacon.' He stared at Robert, challenging his authority.

'You are too late, Molton. I have already written to him, suggesting a marriage match,' Robert challenged.

'Too late,' Ruth spoke for the first time. 'I have secured my future with Samuel and what is done cannot be undone.' She felt Samuel squeeze her hand.

Miss Connelly gasped at the implication in her words and Mrs Fairly quickly found a seat.

'You have acted like a — '

'Eliza!' Robert snapped.

'Excuse us.' Samuel looked at Mrs Fairly. 'I intend to move Miss Grainger into my uncle's home. It has been recently opened, and from there we shall be married once her parents have given us their blessing.'

'What uncle's home?' Robert was almost shouting at them.

'Over Mallow Hall. You may have heard of it, Robert. I believe that you and James need to discuss how it came to be mentioned for sale to Mr Bryant, sir, when my uncle still had residence within its walls.' He stood in front of Robert. 'This conversation, I believe, should take place in private.'

Robert was shocked into silence as he looked at James, who fixed a firm stare on him in return.

'Ladies, if you would care to rejoin the dance, our engagement will be announced shortly.' Ruth led Mrs Fairly, Eliza and Miss Connelly back into the ballroom while the men remained closeted within the library.

19

Mr Upton, somewhat bewildered by his inability to find Ruth, saw her leaving the library and immediately presented himself at her side.

'Oh, Mr Upton,' Mrs Fairly exclaimed, 'Robert needs to see you urgently in the library. I believe it is in connection with concerns from a Mr Bryant.'

Upton's attention left Ruth immediately. He looked towards the doors behind them. 'Miss Grainger, I shall return shortly to speak with you personally. Please do not leave the assembly rooms until we have spoken.'

Ruth did not say anything as he walked away. Eliza glowered at her and returned with Miss Connelly to her previous gathering. To Eliza's annoyance, Mrs Fairly pulled her hand away from her daughter's and stayed with Ruth.

'I know this looks bad, Mrs Fairly,

but I . . . ' Ruth began to speak to the older woman who had always been kind to her.

'Don't make excuses, Ruth.' Mrs Fairly led her to the opposite side of the room to her daughter.

'I am sorry, truly I am. It is not as bad as it may seem.' Ruth looked into her eyes directly, hoping they would not be filled with disappointment and hurt.

'Yes, it is, Ruth, but not because of you, or your young man. Robert has trusted that wretch Upton, and he has brought nothing but shame on my family. Or will do, unless James can intervene in time. To think he would even inflict ruin on a loyal driver! The man knows no humility.' She squeezed Ruth's hand gently. 'Not to worry. You have escaped his threat.'

'You are not angry with me?' Ruth asked, surprised at the woman's behaviour. She had only ever appeared to care about propriety before.

'I would have done the same in your circumstances, but it is a shame you had not told me more beforehand. It could all have been so easily avoided. You see, when I was made aware of the danger Mr Upton posed to my family, it was so easy to help in his downfall. You may not have had to attach yourself to Mr Molton at all.'

Ruth's shock showed.

'Girl, do you not think that I have lived enough years to know when to draw the line? I shall not see my daughter ruined.'

'Why did you not stop me entering the library if you knew we did not need to force an engagement?' Ruth asked, wondering if Samuel would regret his actions when he, too, found out.

'Because I think you both make a handsome couple, and besides, Mr Molton has already written to your father expressing his feelings and honourable intentions towards you. Do you think I should have stopped him now?'

Ruth smiled. 'No, I think you acted wisely.'

'I always do, Ruth. However, now I suggest we rejoin Eliza, and share your good news and fortune.'

'I don't think that I should,' Ruth protested.

'Then on this matter, let me do the thinking for you. You have your good reputation to uphold.'

★　★　★

Upton entered the library and was obviously surprised to see Robert, James, Samuel, and Mr Bryant waiting for him.

'Robert, I was unaware we were having a meeting of sorts. Do you not wish to enjoy the evening with the ladies?' He looked at Bryant. 'Charles, good of you to come. I hope you enjoyed the races.'

'Not at all, my man. I did not take your offer up. Not when I found out where the animal had been stabled and how it was acquired!' Bryant shoved one hand in his pocket.

'I do not understand; I own the stables.' Upton looked furtively at Robert, who was standing next to James, also staring at him.

'Is there some problem, gentlemen, or may I continue to enjoy the ball? I have a pressing *engagement* to announce, do I not, Robert?' He smiled, but Robert did not.

'No, Mr Upton, you do not. Mr Molton has announced his engagement to Miss Grainger. They intend, in time, to live at Over Mallow Hall, his uncle's home.' Robert looked at Samuel, who nodded at him, knowing the man had decided to make a stand with them.

Upton was obviously feeling the chill as Robert's loyalties deserted him. He pointed at Samuel accusingly. 'James, arrest that man! He was the highway robber who stole my deeds. I knew I recognised you from somewhere, you blackguard. I should have seen it earlier.'

'Mr Upton, it is not Mr Molton who is to be arrested. Neither is it Miss Grainger, Mrs Fairly, or the driver who you say recognised Samuel as the high-wayman. The notion is preposterous.'

'Preposterous, is it? You would take the word of a thief, a lovesick girl, and an old woman over that of a gentle-man?' Mr Upton stood to his full height.

'No, but I know our driver has been proved to be of good character — not a thief. Mrs Fairly is a mature lady with astute senses and, regarding Miss Grainger, I hardly think that being in love would blind her judgement when it came to daylight robbery. No, sir, it is you who have twice accused men falsely.' James stood forward, staring the man down. 'It is you who have tried to sell to this man property whose deeds you did not even possess, let alone own, and whose ownership of the stables is equally questionable.'

'Robert, are you going to stand back silently whilst our business partnership is scandalised and questioned?' Upton stared around James at Robert.

'Mr Upton, you have duped me, as

you have these other poor fools. What did you drug my man with? You are beyond the pale, man. And to think I trusted you! Miss Grainger has had a very lucky escape. James, take him away.'

'You bast — '

James stepped forward, but Upton turned and burst through the library doors onto the dance floor. He ran across, knocking into anyone in his path. Samuel went to give chase, but James stopped him. 'My men are outside and guarding his house. They have taken papers from his shop and study. He isn't going far.'

Samuel nodded as the dancers returned to the floor, a new piece being played.

'Robert, a word, please.' James gestured he should remain in the library. Bryant left and Samuel raised an eyebrow at James as Robert went back inside.

'Will he escape untainted?' Samuel asked.

'He can't; his name is on some of the papers and his funds have been used for Upton's dealings. However, I have these papers separated from the others . . . '

'I know how you feel about Eliza, but you can't break the law for him.'

'I don't intend to, but I have bought him a few days' head start. Eliza shall have her divorce, he will not return, and I shall look after Eliza and her mother. Scandal will be kept at arm's length.'

'Thank you, James.' He nodded and entered the library, closing the doors firmly behind him.

★   ★   ★

Samuel interrupted the ladies as he took Ruth onto the dance floor for one last dance before they would leave, together. Mrs Fairly watched them, a smile crossing her face.

'Mother, I do not see what you find so amusing. They have acted appallingly.' Eliza sniffed.

'I see two people in love, and that is a happy thing to witness.'

'Samuel completely ruined Robert's plans for her. He will not be happy about that.'

192

'Oh, I think he will have more to be displeased about than that, Eliza.'

Eliza stared at her mother and looked toward the library, when she saw James. Her face lit up instantly as he came to her and took her onto the dance floor.

Miss Connelly approached Mrs Fairly. 'You seem very happy. Why?'

'I was just watching two people in love,' she repeated as she watched her daughter.

Miss Connelly's eyes were scrutinising Ruth and Samuel as they covered the floor. 'Yes, I can see that. She's completely stolen his heart, lucky girl.' She giggled and winked at her friend.

'Indeed?' Mrs Fairly responded. 'I hadn't seen it that way, but yes, you're quite right. I think she has.'

THE END

MOLLY'S SECRET

CHLOE'S FRIEND

A PHOENIX RISES

ABIGAIL MOOR:
THE DARKEST DAWN

DISCOVERING ELLIE

TRUTH, LOVE AND LIES

SOPHIE'S DREAM

TERESA'S TREASURE

ROSES ARE DEAD

AUGUSTA'S CHARM

We do hope that you have enjoyed reading this large print book.

Did you know that all of our titles are available for purchase?

We publish a wide range of high quality large print books including:
Romances, Mysteries, Classics
General Fiction
Non Fiction and Westerns

Special interest titles available in large print are:
The Little Oxford Dictionary
Music Book, Song Book
Hymn Book, Service Book

Also available from us courtesy of Oxford University Press:
Young Readers' Dictionary
(large print edition)
Young Readers' Thesaurus
(large print edition)

For further information or a free brochure, please contact us at:
Ulverscroft Large Print Books Ltd.,
The Green, Bradgate Road, Anstey,
Leicester, LE7 7FU, England.
Tel: (00 44) **0116 236 4325**
Fax: (00 44) **0116 234 0205**

CALIFORNIA DREAMING

Angela Britnell

When plucky L.A. journalist Christa Reynolds loses her fiancé and her job, she decides it's time for a change of scene. Nearly seventy years ago, her English-born grandmother was evacuated from war-torn London to safety with the Treneague family in Cornwall, and as there's been a standing invitation ever since for the Reynoldses to visit, Christa decides to take them up on it. But she hadn't reckoned on meeting wounded ex-Marine Dan Wilson, and soon she has a life-changing choice to make . . .

SECRET HEARTACHE

Teresa Ashby

Midwife Emma Finch starts work at a new hospital, the Bob, back in her native Yorkshire. It's supposed to be a fresh start for her and her daughter, Keira, but then she discovers that Nick Logan — the man she once loved with all her heart, and who left her when she needed him most — is her department consultant. It soon becomes clear that the old spark between them is still very much alive. Can Emma and Nick reforge a relationship after the heartbreak of the past five years?

THE FIDDLER'S WALTZ

June Davies

In post-war Liverpool, Ellen Butterworth's ambitious sweetheart Brian leaves the Navy and comes ashore so they can begin a future together. An urgent telegram from her younger sister Jeanette interrupts their wedding plans, and Ellen must return to the Yorkshire wool town where she grew up. Unexpectedly, Brian follows her — he wants them to be married there and then in Yorkshire! But, from the moment Jeanette appears in the room, Brian isn't able to take his eyes from her . . .

THE ORCHID

Lucy Oliver

London, 1840: When Ava Miller's father died, she promised she would continue to run The Orchid Theatre and look after its close-knit family of actors. But when Henry Scott-Leigh, the son of the wealthy owner of the theatre, turns up one day threatening to replace Ava or close the unprofitable business altogether, the future looks bleak. Can Ava make a success of the next play and save everything she loves? And what will come of the growing attraction she and Henry share, when they inhabit such different worlds?

TRUST IN ME

Christina Green

Melody Hepworth is made redundant from her job in London, and has parted from her boyfriend. She returns home to the small Devon town where her Aunt Cis runs an antiques business. A lover of vintage clothes, Mel decides to start collecting them again and make a new career, turning the shabby old shop into a sophisticated modern boutique. When she meets attractive local silversmith Rick Martin, there's a spark — but Mel knows she will never trust a man again, let alone allow herself to love him . . .

TOO GOOD TO BE TRUE

Wendy Kremer

The picturesque Canadian village of Pineville provides more than simple holiday relaxation when ex-journalist Amy Watson arrives to visit her relatives. What is she to do when she finds herself falling for hunky Luke, local businessman and environmentalist, when she will be flying back to the UK in just a few weeks? To make matters worse, Luke's beautiful and eminently fashionable fellow environmentalist Jill seems to be determined to win his heart first. Can Amy return to her old life, and leave Luke and Jill to each other?